Stone Skimmers

Stone Skimmers

Jennifer Wisner Kelly

Winner of the G. S. Sharat Chandra Prize for Short Fiction
Selected by Stewart O'Nan

BkMk Press
University of Missouri-Kansas City
www.umkc.edu/bkmk

BkMk Press
University of Missouri-Kansas City
5101 Rockhill Road
Kansas City, MO 64110
www.umkc.edu/bkmk

Executive Editor: Robert Stewart
Managing Editor: Ben Furnish
Assistant Managing Editor: Cynthia Beard

Cover Art: Abby Record, *At the Beach*

Missouri Arts Council

Financial assistance for this book has been provided by the Missouri Arts Council, a state agency.

BkMk Press wishes to thank Chris Arnone, Bethany Graham, Mary Henn, Rhiannon Minster, and Abigail Roberts-Baca. The G. S. Sharat Chandra Prize for Short Fiction wishes to thank Valerie Fioravanti, Leslie Koffler, Linda Rodriguez, and Evan Morgan Williams.

Library of Congress Cataloging-in-Publication Data

Names: Kelly, Jennifer Wisner, 1971- author.
Title: Stone skimmers : stories / Jennifer Wisner Kelly.
Description: Kansas City, MO : BkMk Press/University of Missouri-Kansas City, [2019] | "Winner of the G.S. Sharat Chandra Prize for Short Fiction selected by Stewart O'Nan." | Summary: "The seven stories in Stone Skimmers follow a clique of sheltered teenagers from affluent Old Stonington, Connecticut, a coastal town many choose to leave but none can escape, as they finish high school and launch adult lives. Story subjects include seaside swimming and diving, camping, farming, marriage and divorce, childrearing, accidental death, and memory"-- Provided by publisher.
Identifiers: LCCN 2019024915 | ISBN 9781943491193 (paperback)
Classification: LCC PS3611.E449225 A6 2019 | DDC 813/.6--dc23
LC record available at https://lccn.loc.gov/2019024915

ISBN: 978-1-943491-19-3

This book is set in Versailles LT Std.

Contents

For Tucker

Foreword

The best stories contain an element of strangeness—even the quietest ones. They begin innocently enough. A village gathers on the town green for its midsummer festival. A Saint Bernard chases a rabbit into its warren. No need for someone to wake up and find they've turned into a giant bug, though that can be fun too. Before things turn dire, there's at least a nod to realism, whatever form that may take at the time. It's possible, surely, by some short in the wiring or power surge, that we might hear the voices of our neighbors coming from an enormous radio. It's only when we're eavesdropping on their deepest secrets that we realize we've crossed into the haunted world of the tale.

None of the stories in Jennifer Wisner Kelly's debut advertises itself as outright horror or a detour into the supernatural. They're quiet and intimate—literary fiction, if you absolutely have to pick a genre—drawing us into fraught and off-kilter relationships in isolated settings, yet each turns on an unexplained, often violent disturbance in the lives of its characters.

The initial imbalance is small, and common. It may be the nagging sense of failure that dogs Glenn in "The Catch-and-Release Man" or the everyday frustrations of Adeline, a single mother dealing with teenagers in "Thaw," but these mild discontents are just the beginning.

To reach the castle, as Flannery O'Connor says, you have to pass by the dragon, and like her people, Kelly's heroes have to put their unhappy lives aside and battle forces beyond their understanding, their imperfect worlds suddenly in mortal peril. The mismatched sisters descend into the lightless cave in "El Cenote." The standoffish Nan, in "Sirens," plunges into the cold lake after her crazy great-aunt Celine.

Kelly knows it's when things go out of control that they get interesting. In her universe, nothing is certain, and nothing is easy. Every risk bears serious consequences. Besides a winning intimacy and richness of setting, each story in *Stone Skimmers* possesses a giddy moment of lift, to paraphrase John Gardner, which thrills the reader, who, like her characters, now sees the world in a whole new light. Smart, funny, sad, sharp—this is a marvelous collection. I'm honored to award the 2018 G. S. Sharat Chandra Prize for Short Fiction to Jennifer Wisner Kelly.

—Stewart O'Nan
final judge, G. S. Sharat Chandra Prize for Short Fiction

Stone Skimmers

Stone Skimmers

Old Stonington, Connecticut: 1989

Each night at dusk we built our fire in the usual spot, back from the water's edge, camouflaged by white-barked birches and scraggly pines. We sprawled our bodies across the rocks and logs that encircled this makeshift hearth. Finally, we said, a place of our own.

The town reservoir was broad and held back on the western side by a squat concrete dam. Its deep water had a surreal ability to reflect our many moods: brash, sullen, languid, or golden. Or maybe, we would wonder after a particularly relaxing smoke, maybe our moods were created by the water itself. Chicken or the egg and all that. There was only one beach, belonging to the camp for inner-city kids. Otherwise, swimming was off-limits. The restriction was supposed to keep the water potable, but somehow those interlopers had secured a dispensation. As if their germs wouldn't contaminate the water the way that ours surely would? We figured we had more of a claim to the reservoir than those kids, having lived our whole lives in Old Stonington—a tiny village subsumed within an already inconsequential Connecticut town.

We had been inseparable since our time at the Red Wagon Nursery School, a place our mothers chose not so much for the virtues it espoused (social development, child-driven learning, the power of play) but for the implicit promises it made (Colby, Williams, Harvard—not anywhere in-state, except Yale, of course). Promises that would finally come to fruition in the fall, for the most part, to our mothers' smug satisfaction. Don't ever let it be said, though, that our mothers weren't willing to toil for their children's well-being: at the Red Wagon they had volunteered to scrub miniature toilets and knee-high sinks, feigned enthusiasm for finger painting and sand tables, all for our benefit. Whether or not we would have chosen one another as playmates without our mothers' intervention became as irrelevant over the years as whether we would have chosen our parents or our siblings or Old Stonington itself.

OUR SPOT WAS NEAR the place where a kid we never knew committed suicide, asphyxiating himself in a car. When June wasn't around, we debated the make and model: olive-green Pinto and maroon Monte Carlo were the leading contenders. Oh, we had all heard things. And we weren't afraid to embellish. Fictions we swore were fact. Truths we said our own mothers had told us. For the logistics, we speculated whenever we were unusually bored. He'd stuffed up the tailpipe with an old T-shirt or one of his mother's dish towels. Or, he'd jury-rigged a hose to feed the exhaust directly back into the car to speed up the process. It took five minutes. No, an hour. The better part of a Monday.

We had found our spot back in freshman year while searching for overlooked evidence in a weedy dirt turnout. We certainly weren't the first ones to come—trash strewn around the site made that clear—not the first to crave a mystery, an outlier, an acknowledged failure. Plus, it was the only place at the reservoir where we could ditch a half-dozen bikes or, later, park a car or two and not attract attention from Officer Mino on one of his jaunts.

In the summer, we came to the reservoir during the day, too. Sometimes by ourselves; sometimes June's brother Thomas and his friends would show up to flirt with us, when they had nothing better to do. Or so they said. Thomas chain-smoked his way through these gatherings, indulgent of his friends' immaturity but not inclined to partake. Somewhere in the last two years, Thomas had become an ascetic, denying himself booze and pot and sex and varsity soccer, keeping only nicotine to settle his shakes. Thomas made us all nervous, even June. He made our jokes seem crass, our flirtations juvenile, and our observations dim. Still, we had to love him as one of our own.

We all had tedious part-time jobs that kept us away from the reservoir. Jobs our parents had secured to help us "appreciate our advantages" before we headed off to college. Nevertheless, at any given time, we had a critical mass. Enough people to swim in the amber water, to eat peanut-butter-and-jelly sandwiches and Doritos from the stash of food we kept locked up in a cooler, to skim stones across the water, or to play hearts and strip poker. We contemplated setting up a tent, bringing in sleeping bags, so we could stay in our spot twenty-four hours a day. We didn't push each other on this, though, because really each of us wanted to return to our own hot showers and decent dinners, televisions and stereos, even if our parents were under the same gabled roof. Soon enough there would be shared dorm rooms and hall showers, changes we loudly awaited and quietly feared.

BECAUSE WE WERE SO regular in our habits, we realized that someone else was, too. Every afternoon around three, a girl biked to the opposite side of the reservoir where it abutted Route 18. She would pull on a white bathing cap and stride into the water. She would swim across in a straight line, each day choosing a slightly longer trajectory, her destination a few degrees further clockwise around the perimeter. It was as if she were charting the rays of the sun from that stony spot where she always started. When she reached her day's destination, she would flip-turn and swim back to her starting place, using a stroke that never varied, the same crawl at the same pace. The girl swam when the day called for it: when the sun ricocheted off the reservoir's black surface, and we could make out the campers on the eastern edge cannon-balling from their float. We laughed at their unabashed joy, ignoring the pleasure of this place because it had always belonged to us and, we thought, it always would.

The girl also swam on the gray days, when we huddled in each other's arms and borrowed each other's sweatshirts, building our fire early in the day. She swam on the days when even we didn't show up: when we drove to the state beach or managed to nab enough money from our mothers' purses to go to Boston or Riverside Park, or, better yet, to the house of someone whose parents had gone away. But we knew when we returned to the reservoir that the swimmer had been there in our absence because her trajectory had shifted a few degrees further along the shoreline.

We finally remembered to bring binoculars to watch her getting in and out of the water. She had two Speedo suits, one navy blue with white trim and one with neon-green swirls. And always there was the white cap and a pair of swim goggles. Before she swam, she would stretch out her too-long arms, pulling one, then the other, across her chest, slapping her back, flexing her knees and elbows, stretching and twisting, releasing whatever elastic thing was wound around her core.

The swimmer would leave her towel, flip-flops, and track shorts on a little strip of dirt and swim for an hour—more— and when she was done, she would perch on a small boulder, wrapped up in the towel, and nibble on a sandwich, held fast in her two hands.

As a rule, June and Thomas didn't talk about their sister Anne. Not even right after the funeral. We had all gone to it, of course. First Congregational had been packed, pew on pew. Afterward, at the luncheon, Thomas had smoked a joint in the back garden, the last time he had, as far as any of us could recall. Then he said, *Let's get the fuck out of here.* So we had. After that we never went up the river to the spot where the train bridge spans a shale-lined creek bed. No one, not obsequious Officer Mino or Mr. and Mrs. Stanton and certainly none of us, ever asked Thomas for more than the barest of accountings of that night. And though we speculated, all he had ever told anyone for certain was that Anne had been on the bridge, and then she wasn't. That he had had his eyes closed. *Accident*, everyone declared, because who wanted to consider any reality other than that? We learned to walk around the topic of Anne like it was a quicksand pit. But even if you were careful, you could still tumble into the gaping maw of June and Thomas's pain. You could be entirely innocently talking about some movie you saw or song you hated, and everyone would go quiet because that had been Anne's leading man or her favorite band. Then we would all have to pause and think about it. About the point of impact. About the moment of departure from this world to another. About the overflowing church. About the girls in their floral May Day dresses and the boys in their blazers and Nantucket Red dress shorts, like it was a tea party. And we thought about our mothers in their black shifts and pantyhose, choosing the right necktie for our fathers, both sweating up a rash in the balcony, having surrendered the prime seats to the grieving, party-ready teenagers. We were, frankly, a little tired of it, of all that mourning, and a little relieved whenever the Stantons weren't around so we could stop censoring what came out of our mouths.

AGAIN THE NEXT DAY we watched the girl swim across the reservoir. Arrow-straight. Not once did she look up to mark her bearings. It was supernatural. Not that we were incompetent swimmers, mind you. We had served our time in summer lap lanes, while our mothers absent-mindedly applauded. But this girl wasn't just wasting time until her parents finally called it a night, and she could sneak off to smoke a joint that some friend had gotten from some other friend who had driven into Middletown for it. No, she had a plan.

"It's Evie Callahan," said Alice after a quick look through the binoculars. "She's a sophomore. She's on the swim team."

Alice was stick-skinny and skittish. No one liked her exactly, but she was innocuous and she came with June, so what could we do?

"That's all you've got?" Rita asked.

"Her father teaches math at the academy."

"And?" Rita prompted. Alice only shrugged, but we weren't quite buying her ignorance.

We asked if this Evie Callahan was any good at swimming.

"Yeah, I guess so," said Alice. "On the long distance stuff she's pretty much the best."

This news landed heavily. We wanted the swimmer to be bad, to be dismissible. Alice rubbed her boney arms trying to create a little friction.

"Her mother left, I think," Alice said a moment later, exploring whether this would cheer us. It could be hard to know. Any less-than-traditional family structure could be a plus, and no-mother was a double bonus, but abandonment smacked of pathetic undesirability, and that wouldn't do.

But then Rita said, "Lucky her," and we all nodded our approval of the verdict. We all had mothers, and we all hated them.

Once we had the girl's name and identity, we got to work. And though none of us really knew Evie, we collectively pieced together a memory. First, of her mother. Mrs. Callahan with her big, white teeth and her long, wide smile, which she would flash while proffering a candy bowl at Halloween or a plate of cookies at a party at the academy that we had all been dragged to, or a box of dripping popsicles at the beach on the day school let out. Mrs. Callahan with her pink and green that somehow managed to be garish when our own mothers' Bermuda bags and plaid skirts seemed, if prim, at least tolerable. Mrs. Callahan was from somewhere else: New Jersey or Chicago maybe. Somewhere with rough edges that all her buffing couldn't quite rub away. Maybe that's where she went back to when she left her daughter behind. If we squinted, we could just picture a little girl hiding somewhere behind her mother's skirt on the playground, or over on the porch serving pigs-in-a-blanket on a little tray with her eyes nailed to the floorboards, or sucking her thumb in the cattails at the marina while her father sanded his boat, or dressed up in gauzy white, a child bride on her way to St. Joseph's.

Every afternoon, Evie Callahan made her tick-tock way around the reservoir on some sort of collision course with our spot, and we couldn't help but hate her a little more with each knife-carved stroke and *O*-mouthed suck of air. Motherless or not. Her lean body with its oversized quads and its manly, rounded shoulders. We hated the muscles on her back that didn't belong on any normal fifteen-year-old girl. Her hair cropped short. So when Thomas said, *Just look at her go.* Or, *She's a machine.* Or, *You gotta give her credit.* Or when he shook his head like Evie Callahan was some Olympian, it took a full ten count and at least three good drags to resist slapping him.

"You're into Amazons now?" said Rita, laughing but not meaning it.

Rita was deep into her campaign to win Thomas that summer. When she wasn't around, we would all speculate that she didn't care about him, didn't even like him really, he was just the only guy who had ever turned her down. The rest of them had all succumbed to Rita's charms at least once or twice. Well, except for Sully Faydah. He alone seemed immune to Rita's pheromones. Sully had been Rita's sidekick ever since they had been in the spring musical together. We called him an honorary chick and let him come to the reservoir whenever he wanted.

It wasn't just Rita, of course. We had fooled around with each other. By that point we were running out of combinations. We'd already double- or even triple-dipped. Occasionally someone would look outside of our circle and try to bring in a new person, but it never worked. They always felt like a fake limb. We had to explain all the inside jokes to them. They were always wearing that glued-on smile. Or, worse yet, they thought that they could slot right in. As if the decade and a half that had cemented the rest of us together didn't matter.

We speculated on how long it would be before Evie Callahan's swimming trajectory would lead right to our spot. A week. Maybe two? Some of us began to wonder if all around the reservoir Evie Callahan had been stumbling into groups just like ours: isolated clutches believing they were alone, like little populated planets ignorant of all the other life out there in the universe. It made us shudder to imagine that Evie Callahan knew something we didn't.

In the end, it was Rita, of course, who finally got the scoop on the reservoir suicide. Her little sister had heard the story from an older cousin who could be counted on for reliable Old Stonington trivia. Rita held onto this nugget until a day when June had to work and Thomas was caddying for their father, then she announced haughtily that we'd gotten it all wrong, as if *she* hadn't been part of *we*. It turned out that the boy had been local. And popular. Eight years older than us. It was his father's butter-yellow Mercedes. *A big, fat fuck-you,* to use Rita's expression. She told us that the kid's parents couldn't keep the car after what had happened, but they couldn't sell it either because the fumes had permeated the upholstery so deeply. It seemed blasphemous to lie about why they'd want to get rid of the car, so in the end, they had to sell it for scrap. Rita laughed, declaring it a righteous penance for asshole parents. She was so hostile that even we doubted if we should chime in. June once said that Rita reminded her of those prickly horse chestnuts that we used to throw at the boys on the playground in the fall. *Those prickles,* she said, *made you think that they must be protecting something all soft and squishy, but when you finally got the stupid thing open, there was just that smooth, hard nut.*

OUR MOTHERS LIKED TO leave the *Gazette* on the breakfast table for us. They would already be on the eighth hole or sipping iced tea courtside or pruning the roses by the time we dragged ourselves from our nests. They clipped articles we were expected to read: honor rolls, wedding announcements, sports scores. All that endless achievement. They circled tidbits and wrote in the margins: *Isn't that the girl from dance class?,* or *Who knew?!,* or *Thought you'd be interested.* We had all had our share of mentions in the *Gazette.* Team victories. Finish lines. Curtain calls. Best. Top. First. But there had also been Honorable Mentions, Not Pictureds, and Minors Found in Possession.

No fewer than three of us brought the fifth page of that week's *Gazette* to the reservoir.

Local Girl Takes Plunge for Charity.

There was a picture of Evie Callahan, and even in newsprint black and white, we recognized her suit as the green one. She had taken off her swim cap, thankfully, and stood between two men. One was Coach Carver from our school team; the caption told us the other was Mr. Callahan. Together, they held an enormous cardboard check. You'd have expected Evie to be smiling, what with ten thousand dollars for charity and a photographer staring her down. The two men were. But not Evie. She was straight-faced, her eyes focused a hair away from the camera, like someone or something had caught her eye just as the shutter clicked.

Sully's mother had written: *What a great idea!* Alice's wrote: *From swim team?*

Someone read: *Well-wishers can see her off on Friday, August 25th at Daunton's Marina at dawn.*

"She probably won't make it," said Rita. "It's like ten miles across."

What was the point, we wondered. Swimming across Long Island Sound. All that training and for what? Who cares?

"She's just doing it for her college applications," someone said, because what hadn't we all done with the Ivy League in mind?

"Yeah, maybe," the rest of us said, knowing it wasn't true.

Through the trees, we could make out Evie completing her third hour of swimming for the day. Her stealthy stroke was as robotic and perfect as usual, her arms and feet barely noticeable above the gold-tipped ripples of the water. Not once did she roll onto her back and let the hungry sun take away the reservoir's cold. We reminded each other that we'd have to be vigilant if we wanted to catch her arrival at our spot.

WE WERE STARTING TO realize, each one of us in our own time, that Evie was an early arrival from the rest of our lives. She was the kind of person we would meet in September, people we would cut our adult teeth on, who wouldn't play according to the carefully carved rules that we had negotiated in our first eighteen years. Who weren't older or younger versions of ourselves, living identical Old Stonington lives in perpetuity. And even though she was two years younger and probably not ever going to escape the town the way that we were about to—breaking free of all its damn traditions and habits and expectations—if we had been honest with each other, we would have admitted that Evie's briny blend of sadness and self-confidence and intensity intoxicated us. We already knew everything each of us was willing to share and quite a few things we stupidly considered sacrosanct, not realizing the others already knew anyway. Confidences had been breached, letters and diaries read, conversations overheard. We were, above all else, bored. And then, into that vacuum, swam Evie Callahan.

WE BOUGHT CONES AT Macintyre's while Rita scooped, waiting around for her shift to end. When she finally came out the bent screen door of the shack, she held an enormous ice cream tub over her head in victory. It was nearly empty and we had to dig in up to our armpits to get anything. Never mind that we had already eaten our fill of the stuff while waiting for Rita. We pushed at each other to get another spoonful and licked drips off each other's arms. We pretended it was just about the ice cream, but we stole glances at Thomas and the other guys to see if our tantalizing lesbian act was turning them on. They followed us as we walked down the streets of Old Stonington with that tub raised. We were royalty with plastic spoons for staffs.

We didn't say we were headed to the Callahans' house, but somehow our sugar rush took us out of town, past the church and the old graveyard where we usually stopped for a little sacrilegious hang-out time until one of the roly-poly town cops would send us on our way.

The Callahans lived in a particularly pretty faculty bungalow, white with dark green shutters in the New England way. There was a light on in each of the upstairs rooms: one had open blinds and the other floral curtains, so we presumed to know which was Evie's and which was her father's. We could have been direct and rung the bell, but there was too much legitimacy in that kind of social call. We didn't know exactly what we wanted from Evie Callahan, but her approval and friendship weren't on the list.

"C'mon," said Thomas. "Let's get out of here."

Even the other guys ignored him, and no one objected when he proclaimed us all losers and started his solitary trek back to town.

The rest of us snuck down the driveway commando-style and hid behind a beat-up station wagon. We threw tiny, sharp pebbles at the floral-curtained window. They rattled on the glass panes and then down the porch roof. We shushed each other.

Evie appeared at the other lit window, and we thrilled at our mistake. She looked out into the night, head cocked. We squatted down until our quads ached, unable to kneel on the sharp stones. Evie raised the blinds and the screen and leaned out. She wore a thin cotton nightgown and with the light behind her, we saw even more of her body than at the reservoir. She looked above us, past us, to the backyard, to the star-thick sky. Our breathing was deep and impossibly loud, but if Evie noticed the collective beast stalking her, she was unfazed. She slid back inside and shut off the light.

We stood to leave, disappointed, and spotted Mr. Callahan stretched out on a lounge chair in his backyard, not more than fifteen feet from us, nursing a tumbler. We followed his eyes skyward and spotted a star plummeting, and then another and another. Yet another. We pointed and poked each other in hushed exhilaration. Wishes granted for each of us over and over again.

"Evie?" Mr. Callahan hollered toward the open screen door.

We froze and ducked behind the car again. A moment later, Mr. Callahan called out a second time, but then only loud enough for us to hear, certainly not audible to his daughter in the front bedroom at the top of the stairs with her door closed: "Come quick," he said. "You're missing it."

And his longing was so plain that we prayed Evie would say back: "I'm here. I see them. They're glorious." But nothing stirred inside the bungalow.

Once we realized that there was nothing but inky night between us and the Callahans and whatever pain they harbored, we snuck back through the holly bushes and made our silent way home.

THE SECOND FRIDAY IN August we holed up at June and Thomas's house because a hurricane was coming, and even we didn't like our spot enough to ride out gale-force winds there. Their house was next door to Sully's, two doors down from Rita's, and around the corner from Alice's. They were all enormous, nineteenth-century temples of excess with multiple staircases and attic rooms to accommodate the underclass, but in 1989 they accommodated us. June had the entire third level to herself, and we waited out the storm on her bed and beanbag chairs, rain raucous against the slate roof. Thomas didn't have the rest of his posse with him, but he must have been bored enough to join us upstairs, leaning against the doorframe, unwilling to commit.

Maybe it was the intimacy of being inside with the furious sky outside, but that afternoon tantalized us to confess whatever we were holding precious. Alice succumbed first. She lived on the periphery of our circle and took advantage of any opportunity to buttress her tenuous status.

This is what she told us:

"You know how me and Evie were on the swim team together last year? Well, she turned up at try-outs like she had just moved here from out of town or something when, of course, she's been here the whole time, just like us. Then after one length of the pool she had, like, a good two yards on everybody, even the seniors."

We wanted to know where she had learned to swim like that: It certainly wasn't at the club pool with the rest of us.

"Who knows," said Alice, swatting us away like a gnat. "That's not the point."

She reached out for one of Thomas's cigarettes, the knobs of bone at her knuckles and wrist as pronounced as marbles. We watched her elbow and shoulder joints roll in their sockets when she brought the cigarette up for a drag. It was impossible to not let revulsion show on our faces, so we looked away from the spectacle she was becoming.

When Alice wasn't there, we talked about her evaporation. How little she was eating. The bathroom sounds. We called it disgusting. Rita could touch her thumb to her index finger around Alice's forearm. No, her biceps. It was impossible not to think of the pictures in our history textbook. Dachau. Auschwitz. What we never admitted was that in the privacy of our bedrooms we considered our own fleshy bits. Pinching. Rating. We envied Alice's self-restraint. We asked our mothers to add cottage cheese and Tab to the shopping list. They made no objection. We touched our tongues to the curdled white mess and secretly tossed it. Next time we asked for grapefruit or iceberg lettuce or Special K.

"Keep listening," Alice said with irritation, and we did because it was better than having to confess our own secrets.

Then she told us that maybe because Evie was an only child like her, or maybe because Alice never really cared about swimming anyway, or maybe because Evie had the most perfect stroke Alice could imagine—but whatever the reason, Alice had fallen a little in love with Evie, in love with her single-mindedness. With the way she would twang the elastics on the leg openings of her bathing suit. With the way she shook water from her hair and smacked her skull to empty out her ear canals.

We got quiet and exchanged low glances, but then Alice said, "No, no. It wasn't like that."

We began to lose interest. We could count on Alice to say she was in love with a girl and then claim it was just a metaphor.

Not that we believed her denial entirely. We would debate it later, but at that moment Alice still had the floor. Emboldened by the silence she had created, punctuated only by the skitter of branches and rain against glass, she continued. She had been so taken by, so drawn to, Evie Callahan that Alice had begun to smile at her at practice, to offer an encouraging word. And so it was that when everyone else left the pool deck before the final heat, it would only be Alice who stuck around to see Evie snag some new record. Only Alice who witnessed all of Evie's victories. Only Alice who saw Coach Carver pick Evie up and spin her around and plant a big kiss on the crown of her head. And because she had made a study of Evie and seen the stillness in her face, the determination unsullied by joy, only Alice could tell that something about Coach Carver and the kiss was not quite right.

"So," we asked, "you're saying Coach Carver is fucking Evie Callahan?"

"No. I'm just saying there was something weird about it."

Alice's noncommittal answer convinced no one. We labeled it appalling or sexy or creepy: we couldn't agree. Coach Carver was not exactly a dirty old man. Some of us contended that Coach Carver was, in fact, cool. He had that outrageous swimmer's body. On the other hand, he was married with two little kids at home, and there was obviously something wrong with his son. You could see it in the family picture he kept in his office at the pool, as if that made whatever he was up to with Evie somehow worse. Or, some of us said, better—taking pity on a beleaguered man.

"I've heard rumors about him before," Rita said. "There was a girl in my cousin's class. She's at Yale now. But everybody knew about it. He gave her rides home in that nasty pink hatchback."

We all came up with a tidbit to offer, true or not. Who thought Coach Carver had eyes that lingered. Who thought Evie must have seduced him. Who had heard that the coach had been spotted holding hands with *some* girl in the parking lot. Only Thomas wouldn't play. From the doorway he called us obnoxious gossips, first in jest, but when we didn't stop, then again with sincerity.

"We're just talking, Tommy," said June.

Thomas pointed at his sister. Didn't we even care that maybe this poor girl was getting taken advantage of? That maybe she didn't want it? Maybe she lay awake and wept about it because assholes like us couldn't see what was right in front of our fucking noses?

We rolled our eyes. Thomas had obviously been paying too close attention in peer advocacy class.

"She's a nut job," said Rita. "It's obvious. C'mon, Thomas, just admit it."

We never argued like this. Never exposed our raw spots to public view. It was against our rules. Our parents' rules. Old Stonington's rules. So while we waited for Thomas to let go of whatever rage had seized him, we searched June's room for a distraction but found nothing.

Thomas said to us all, so quietly we had to strain to listen above the pounding rain, "It could've been you."

He left then with June chasing behind to make amends. The rest of us avoided eye contact. We shuffled a deck of cards while we waited for June to return, but the argument had settled around the room like soot. So when the eye of the storm passed over us a half hour later, and the wind died to nothing, with the sky still holding its electric charge and glowing a sickly gray-yellow, we decided to decamp to Rita's house. We snuck down the back stairs, ran down the road, skipped past downed branches and healthy green leaves torn from the trees, and hollered a prayer that no live wires were hidden in the puddles.

THE NEXT DAY SULLY drove a bunch of us around town. We still felt a resistance about going to the reservoir, as if the day before would still be whipping up the water and making branches snap. Our mothers told us to watch ourselves. We stuck closer to civilization. Thomas and June hadn't wanted to come, of course, but we said they needed to see what the storm hath wrought, and they finally relented. We bought a dozen donuts and covered ourselves in powdered sugar and glaze. We cruised along the seawall looking for signs of storm damage. The air was dense with salt; it coated the windshield. We saw small boats skewered on pilings and a few areas where the wall had been washed away. The ocean had emptied itself of trash. Piles of Styrofoam and flip-flops and lobster traps and life jackets and old sneakers littered the beach. At the end of the seawall, where the breakwater protected the beach from the open ocean, where the playground stopped and the Atlantic staked its claim, Evie's blue ten-speed rested against the concrete wall.

"Stop! Stop the car," screeched Rita.

Sully hit the brakes, and we stared a long while at Evie's bike. The car shuddered a little when a lonely gust blew past.

"Leave her alone," said June.

Rita said we weren't going to do anything to her.

We paraded, single file, along the seawall, reluctant Thomas bringing up the rear. The sugary taste in our mouths gave way to rank sea salt. We spotted Evie at the end of the breakwater. She was wearing her usual lime-green suit, track shorts, and sneakers. She reached her hands into the air and held the stretch. She windmilled her arms.

The ocean was raucous from the storm, exploding against the boulders into plumes of white water. The breakwater was doing its job. The sound of that work, the deep throttling pounding, proved just how much energy it takes to shred something fluid, liquid, and eternal.

Evie bent forward in a diving pose, like she was on the starting block.

"Jesus," someone said, "she isn't going to dive, is she?"

Even at high tide this was not the best place to dive. There were boulders that had tumbled down from the breakwater. You had to be able to skim the water. In rough weather like this it would be treacherous.

"Maybe we should go get her," said June. "I mean, it really is dangerous."

"Shut up, June," said Rita. "Let's see what she does. We aren't her babysitters."

Evie stood up again and then hopped in place for a few seconds like she was warming up. There was something so vulnerable about her. She clearly didn't know we were watching, she was so wholly absorbed in her fantasy. It was mesmerizing.

Then she turned to face straight into the wind, spotting her finish line on Long Island. Or maybe it was farther than that: England, or Africa, or no finish line at all, just a watery forever.

She stretched her arms wide and leaned into the resistance of the wind. Then gradually, so much so that we didn't notice it at first, she started to flap her arms. They rode the wind, arcing upward, and she pulled them down. Up and down she went. The way we once did at the Red Wagon when we pretended to be airplanes or fairies. Her face was intense with her effort.

"Holy shit," said Sully. "This is fucking hilarious."

"Shh," we all said back.

We watched for several minutes. Evie became balletic in her pantomime. The gull—or whatever it was that she thought she was becoming—soared, rode imaginary thermals, dove for prey. Her feet were light on the slick boulders, traipsing over them with little hops and leaps and spins.

"Look at her," said Thomas. "Look at her go."

Evie could not have been more naked before us. Her exuberance, her inhibition, her innocence were all stripped to their essence. We had finally seen her exposed.

Twice June said she was leaving, only to stay.

"I'm going down there," said Thomas. His eyes were wide.

"No, don't," we all said.

We were losing our nerve.

Thomas swooped off the seawall, landing hard on the sand, falling to his knees and then his hands.

"Tommy," June shouted, but he ignored her.

He stumbled against the wind and over the rocky beach onto the end of the breakwater. He moved awkwardly, tumbling and slipping, coming close to falling into the sharp crevices between the granite slabs, and as he ran, he flapped his arms. He was hollering something, but we couldn't make it out above the wind and the water. Evie heard him, though, and turned. She didn't stop her avian performance. If anything, she stretched her long neck skyward and for that moment she was a bird.

We left Thomas there. All of us, even June, running back down the seawall to the car, cramming in and driving away, holding our breath until there was not even a tendril of connection between us and those two fools.

FOR ALL OF OUR anticipation, Evie's arrival at our spot the following week turned out to be a nonevent. She got within thirty feet of shore, flipped over like she was at the end of the pool and began to swim away.

"Hey," Rita called. "Hey, you!"

When she still didn't turn, Sully blasted one of his signature whistles, so shrill that we had to clamp our hands over our ears. Evie popped up and treaded water, looking around like a startled otter.

She swam closer and stood up, her feet sinking into the muck at the water's edge, peering into the woods. She didn't seem to mind the way the mud squeezed through her toes. She also didn't seem to mind her near nakedness, her projecting nipples, and the water falling from every bit of her.

We crossed our arms over our own chests in silent instruction to this newcomer. Evie either didn't notice or didn't care. She didn't even pull the horrible cap off her head. Her only nod to social norms was to raise her dark goggles onto her forehead, their straps dangling alongside her face, her eyes raccooned from their suction. *Here's what you should do,* we secretly wanted to say to her. To guide her back to normalcy. She was a pretty girl. Now that she was close we could see that. Prettier than some of us. She could be one of us. An energy moved among us that we could all read. She was okay. She could be okay. She could be a worthy project. We needed fresh blood. But Evie didn't pick it up. Her hands rested alongside her body, still as stones. Only her eyes moved, flit-flitting to each of ours.

Evie squinted into the afternoon sun as if she was checking the time, then turned back toward the other side of the reservoir.

"Good luck," June called after her. Evie flapped her hand behind her without turning around, so we knew she had heard us.

When she got to the other side, Evie sat on her rock and ate her snack as methodically as usual. She seemed to have forgotten we were even there. She licked her fingers clean and pulled on her shorts and T-shirt. She didn't even take off the swimming cap until she was ready to go.

Sully and Rita watched her through the binoculars and reported back in a running commentary, dissecting every movement of the girl's body.

Then June said, "Give me the binoculars." After a long look, she said a little wistfully, "Tommy's there."

"Let me see," said Rita.

But even without binoculars we recognized Thomas's tall boy hunch and his red Cornell T-shirt as he walked over to Evie's rock.

"Fucking Thomas," said Rita, and we nodded in silent agreement. He could have her. We told each other that we weren't sad to see him go.

Evie didn't swim at the reservoir again. Instead we saw Thomas's jeep and her bike down at the public dock every morning. We guessed she was practicing in the ocean, getting ready for the big swim.

On the following Thursday evening, we prowled the marina and spotted Mr. Callahan in his docksiders and khaki shorts, with his eraser-pink head, standing at the helm of a Boston Whaler on the refueling dock. He tapped his dials and ran his hand back and forth over his shiny pate.

"We're starting here and landing around Greenport," he said to the dock boy.

"What's that, sir?"

Mr. Callahan pointed across the harbor. He said, "Evie's headed to Greenport tomorrow morning."

"Well, we'll give her a good send-off, sir. When do you think she'll land?"

"Dinner maybe. If she sticks it out, that is. The jellyfish are pretty thick this year."

"Hey, did you hear about that shark they spotted off Montauk?"

Mr. Callahan leaned over his captain's wheel and exhaled loudly. The dock boy quickly added, "Well, there are always sharks. It's no big deal."

"Of course not," Mr. Callahan snapped. "You've got a higher probability of getting killed by lightning than a shark."

We wanted to laugh at this nervous, nerdy man, but we hadn't considered the risks. The jellyfish. The sharks. The other boats. The water so cold. The number of hours it would take to swim across a body of water with no land in sight. The undeniable bravery required to dive from Daunton's dock at dawn. We hadn't really thought about Evie's father, either.

The mathematician without a wife, a fish-girl for a daughter. The two of them traveling in their separate, silent orbits. When had we ever seen them having dinner at Mario's? Or at Macintyre's? Or even driving around together? Sure, we hadn't wanted to be at any of those places with our own sorry clans, but we hadn't had much choice. Even that summer— that final summer that belonged to us more than any three months ever had before or since—there had still been club soirees and send-off parties and Fourth of July barbeques. We hadn't thought about the Callahans. Not really. Whether the long-lost wife and mother would make an appearance in the morning. Whether this was Evie's pathetic attempt to reunite the irreconcilable. Whether all of this was a beginning or an end.

"Well," said Rita, clapping her hands together. "I gotta get to Macintyre's."

"I should pack," said June.

Alice had promised her mother one last awkward family dinner.

The rest of us followed suit, making our excuses and going our separate ways down the streets of Old Stonington.

MAYBE ONE OF US spent that August night in the woods at the reservoir and picked up our trash and our treasures and said goodbye to the copper water and the bubble gum sky. Maybe someone showed up in the morning to cheer on Evie Callahan in her marathon swim. Maybe someone even went along with Thomas on the boat to help out. Maybe someone's mother checked the *Gazette* the next week for a picture of Evie. Maybe someone didn't think about Evie twice on the way out the door to her father's car, waiting to drive her to the future. Maybe someone went down to the beach under the bulging summer moon and counted how many jellyfish were in the water and on the beach, how many toxic red ones and how many harmless white. Maybe someone ran the numbers, made a prediction, placed a wager on what would come next, on who would win, who would lose, who would be first, who last, on who would end up just where she intended, and who would end up right back where we all had started.

Thaw

Adeline can smell snow from twelve hours away. She can smell piecrust five minutes from burning. She can smell rust in water and blood in wood. But like all gifts, this one comes at a cost—there is no stink that Adeline can escape. Today's warm weather has let loose the foul farm smells that winter usually hides: oil from the blacktop driveway softening in the sun, mildew on wet straw, roadkill on Route 79, and chicken shit, always chicken shit. When Adeline steps onto the porch, the smells assault her nostrils. It is tempting to run inside and hide beneath the yeasty aroma of baking bread and the staunch cleanliness of Clorox, but weather this warm doesn't come to northern Vermont in February unless God is showing some mercy, and Adeline needs any mercy on offer. It has been a long winter of silent perseverance. She has waited for storms to pass. For snow to stop falling. For the phone to ring. The letter to come. The queasiness to subside. Today Adeline will wait at the mailbox for the school bus, something she hasn't done since November, but has decided to do now in honor of the weather, in honor of good omens. She hopes to make her little Lizzy smile. A rogue northerly gust sneaks down the open collar of Adeline's sweater, chilling her clavicle, her nipples, her navel, like snow wriggling under your clothes in a snowball fight. It reminds her that today's temperatures are just a tease. You can't count on spring until May.

Hutch gets off the bus first with Lance Stone's boy, a developing relationship that Thomas said they should nip in the bud, but the school isn't big enough for them to dictate Hutch's friends. Maybe there will be better choices when he switches to the regional high school next year. Maybe not. Still, you don't move back to a town like this and expect the other kids to be well-heeled intellectuals. Here their children will have to navigate in the real world, full of real people. Sure, some of those "real" kids are potheads shooting BBs at cans behind Jackson's Grille. But some will go to Ivy League colleges and marry rich boys. Adeline knows all about that possibility. Her own escape had been lucky. And though she held no romantic ideals of what Ashbury was all about, she had gone along with Thomas's plan to move back to her hometown five years ago. Yes, she had agreed, the benefits of a rural childhood would outweigh the dangers, especially when the home environment could be so rich. Both of them would be there all the time, full of their loving-kindness. It was a return to simplicity. Adeline tells herself that the Stone boy will be fine for Hutch. Adeline has known his father all her life. Lance Stone had played football in high school, but six shoulder dislocations in two years took college off the table. Instead, he started a job at Gesky's gas station and managed to buy out the old man a few years before Adeline moved back with Thomas. Lance wasn't a bad guy, then or now. He was an Ashbury guy. His son surely was just more of the same.

Hutch and the Stone boy, whom everyone calls Stony, shuffle past Adeline up the driveway deep in quiet conversation. Hutch lifts his hand in a limp salute and says, "Hey" without making eye contact. To Adeline, this new standoffishness suggests illicit behavior, though Thomas would say that's just where boys are at this age. They don't need their mothers knowing everything they're up to.

Lizzy gets off the bus wearing her trademark glazed expression behind lopsided glasses and a crooked smile for which Adeline takes credit. Lizzy greets the world enthusiastically, but with a tad of confusion, like a newly arrived exchange student. She's ten but looks younger, partly because she's inherited Thomas's slight build over Adeline's sturdy one, and partly because of her quirky way of being in the world. When they first moved back, when Lizzy was only five, Adeline's mother started calling her Baby Bird. Thomas thought it was a term of endearment, but Adeline knew it to be a criticism. To Adeline's mother, there was nothing less appealing than a weak, dependent creature begging for worm after worm.

Today Lizzy has tied her pink windbreaker around her hips and mounted her backpack on both of her boney shoulders. It's heavily laden with reference books from Thomas's study that Lizzy insists on hefting to and from school each day—a hardcover dictionary and thesaurus, a world atlas. All that lugging is probably causing her back all sorts of trouble, but Adeline has decided it isn't worth arguing about.

Adeline wants to gather her daughter into the safe place under her outstretched arm, but before she finishes kissing the top of Lizzy's head, inhaling the lemon smell of her frazzled hair, Lizzy shrugs off both her mother and her backpack.

"I need to feed my chickens," she says, leaving the bag at Adeline's feet and running ahead down the long driveway, past the boys, who punch each other in the biceps as they walk toward the house. Adeline wants to comment on this minor violence but doesn't, heeding Thomas's old admonitions to give the boys some space for God's sake. When Lizzy veers right, Adeline follows, taking a shoveled path that leads across the barnyard to the chicken coop, snow still piled waist high on both sides. Lizzy's jacket wriggles loose and lands on the snow-packed, slushy path. If Adeline weren't pulling up the rear, it would be left there, just another piece of flotsam requiring replacement.

Halfway to the coop, Adeline picks up a new scent: a familiar, raunchy smell. Musk. Fox. She mentally traces it down the slope from the house and the big barn, past the chicken coop and farther down to the woodshed. The smell seems nearly visible, like the poisonous green vapors in the cartoons Lizzy watches on Saturday mornings, the same ones Adeline once watched. Having spent most of her life on the farm, Adeline knows the rules: if there is a fox, there is some delectable thing to keep him around, trash cans without lids or mice or a broken latch on the henhouse. If she wants to get rid of him, she'll have to get rid of whatever it is that keeps him interested. Or she could kill him.

Adeline catches up to Lizzy at the henhouse where Lizzy is admiring her two-dozen heritage-breed chickens that seem to have gotten in the spirit of the warm weather and have ventured into the yard. Thomas built the coop for Lizzy last spring. It's a misnomer to call it a coop, really, since the ground it encompasses is vast enough for the chickens to be considered free-range. The coop is made entirely of sustainable, green materials and like everything else Thomas has built on the farm—the greenhouse, the seed-packaging building, the extraction shed —it's better insulated and more stylish than their house. Thomas never spares any expense. Everything he touches shows a flourish of modern design but still manages to look harmonious with their two-century-old post-and-beam barn and whitewashed farmhouse. Maybe in another life, the one his parents had expected for him, Thomas would have been an architect. Even his favorite motto sounds more like an architect than a farmer: *First, be functional; then, be beautiful.* Adeline wonders whether he ever applied it to her. Surely not anymore, after so many years. But once? She reaches for Lizzy's hand where it clings to the chicken-wire gate. Lizzy lets Adeline hold the soft, warm appendage for a moment before burying both hands in the hip pockets of her jeans.

Adeline succumbs to the urge to check on the boys. They are lingering up there on the wide, covered porch that runs along the back of the house. They are deep in conversation about God knows what, hands flying. Hutch must be explaining something. He's wearing his intense professor face.

Adeline whispers to Lizzy, "Hey, I think there might be a fox down in the woodshed."

Lizzy stays focused on her chickens as if she hadn't heard Adeline. On the other hand, she doesn't open the latch on the coop door to get to work the way she usually would. She must be considering.

Adeline says, "Wanna check it out?"

When Lizzy doesn't move, Adeline gives her a moment longer to process. It's best not to rush Lizzy. "Hey, Hutch," Adeline yells, "you notice a fox in the woodshed?"

"No," Hutch hollers back, his voice not hiding his irritation. He rubs his hand back and forth over his already messy hair.

It has been Hutch's job this winter to bring up wood for the family-room stove and to keep rodents at bay in all the outbuildings. It's a lot of work for a boy, but Adeline needed the help, plain and simple. Of course, the rodents would be easier to kill with poison instead of mousetraps. That's the way her family had always done it. There's still a big box of bait in the barn somewhere, but Thomas won't tolerate toxins on their farm. Not even in the attics or fieldstone basements or other ancient hidey-holes where vermin like to set up house. Adeline has honored this preference during his absence. She figures if she holds true to his way of doing things, he might be more inclined to pick up where he left off when he comes back. If he comes back. Adeline shelves this thought for the third or fourth time today.

"You've been setting traps, right?" she calls up to Hutch. Yelling across the expanse between house and barn seems ridiculous, clearly they should discuss this later, but Adeline wants to embarrass Hutch a little. Make him acknowledge that she is in charge, even with Stony over.

"What?" he says.

"You did the traps?" Adeline yells back.

"Yeah." His voice cracks, and both boys laugh. Then, he says something to Stony, and the two disappear into the house. Adeline doesn't even know that boy's real name. Maybe Stony Stone *is* his real name. Would Lance Stone be so ridiculous?

Now that they are close to the source of the smell, the musk is thick, and Adeline feels like she is breathing through old burlap. She pinches her nostrils shut and breathes asthmatically through her mouth instead. Lizzy is unfazed. "Where is it?" she asks loudly.

"Shh. You'll scare it."

Adeline doesn't really expect to see a fox in their woodshed in the middle of the afternoon, but the traps need checking anyway, and she shouldn't send Lizzy inside with only the boys to supervise her.

The woodshed is not really a shed at all but an oversized root cellar from back when Adeline's grandmother canned anything growing on the farm, intentionally planted or not, and sold it to anyone she could get to buy it, mostly tourists heading down Route 79 who were suckers for farm stands. Three sides of the woodshed are buried underground, walled with fieldstones and floored with dirt, but because the cellar was built into the steep slope of the hill, the lowest side has double, wooden barn doors that open onto a level yard, a place to cut logs and store them until they are dry enough to split. The re-commissioned root cellar holds six cords of wood if you stack tightly. Enough for one regular winter. They stack a couple more cords under tarps outside the shed just in case. From the house, all you can see of the shed is a small mound of earth and the granite lintel of the doorframe. In winter, the woodshed becomes entirely camouflaged by snow.

Sure enough, the dozen mousetraps have been raided and lie around the shed like shipwrecked schooners. By the level of dust, it's likely been weeks or months since the last time the traps saw cheese or peanut butter. Hutch will hear about it over dinner. Really, is a little help so much to ask?

A rustle comes from the back wall of the shed, at the end of the tidy row of firewood that they are currently consuming, wagonload by wagonload. Adeline sees a twitching nose before the creature freezes. She freezes, too. It would make sense to scare the thing away. To assert some humanity over it. But something in Adeline can't resist wanting to see it up close.

Lizzy screeches. The fox doesn't run, but takes a step back before freezing again. Adeline grabs Lizzy by the wrist, hard. "No," she snaps. Then she sugars it up: "If you're too loud, he'll run away, sweetie."

The fox crouches smaller against the back wall, his oversized ears pricked, his nose recognizing their smell as much as Adeline recognizes his. His shoulders flinch, and his copper fur catches a fragment of the tired afternoon light bleeding through the open shed doors. His radiance vibrates. Adeline squats, fully expecting the fox to bolt, but he only watches her. His eyes seem more inquisitive than fearful. Impulsively, she stretches out her hand. He moves toward it.

She waits for the fox to come to her. He moves slowly, his dainty paws lifted in an exaggerated tiptoe. It's a good ten feet from where Adeline squats to the fox's position along the back wall. Adeline has never been so close to a wild thing for so long. Her father and grandfather brought home their share of venison or raccoon or even foxes like this one, but women didn't get involved with hunting and trapping, so she only met these creatures once they were dead and no longer animals but carcasses.

The fox holds up his paw like he wants Adeline to shake. She stretches out her palm and the fox sniffs it, his hot breath tickling and goose-pimpling the flesh of Adeline's inner wrist. Her mouth has filled with saliva from the way she is breathing and her tongue tastes of metallic earth. She swallows hard and then takes a cautious breath through her nose. She expects that the musk stench will be overwhelming, but it is only a mellow tang now, nearly appealing.

The fox steps past Adeline and moves to Lizzy who has flattened herself against the doorframe. He puts a tentative paw on Lizzy's slush-covered boot. She sucks in air and her leg spasms. The fox retreats a few paces.

"Don't move," says Adeline.

"Get it away," hisses Lizzy.

"He won't hurt you."

"It's wild. It's got rabies."

"Shh."

They wait in silence until the fox starts to sniff Adeline's outstretched hand again. He puts his snout against her fingertips. He could bite her. He probably will bite her. He probably does have rabies. Why else would he be out in the middle of the day like this? Or maybe some lonely farmer tamed him, but then the fox got restless and escaped and now here he is, in Adeline's woodshed looking for attention. Who knows. The fox gives quick, rough licks, tasting her. His tongue flicks on the soft webs between her widely spread fingers.

From the porch, Hutch hollers at maximum volume: "Can we eat these cookies, Ma?"

The fox goes rigid again at the voice and then bolts behind cords of stacked wood, lost in the shadows. "Shit," says Adeline.

"Banned word, Mama," says Lizzy, cheerful now that the fox is gone.

"Lizzy..."

"Banned word. No dessert."

"Cut it out."

Adeline walks out of the woodshed and up the hill until she has a clear view of the back porch. Hutch leans over the railing, while Stony rocks himself slowly on the porch swing hung deep in the shade so some field-weary person could hide from the scorch of July. To Adeline, the boy is nothing but a shadow in motion, as if the swing moves of its own haunted accord. She can think only of her own mother rocking on that swing with a bowl of peas for shelling. Or her grandmother with her constant needles: knitting, crocheting, tatting, mending, always making something from only a little thread of nothing.

Adeline doesn't speak until she has made her way up the hill, past the coop where Lizzy heads to feed her chickens, to the bottom of the porch steps.

"So, can we have the cookies?" says Hutch.

Adeline is winded when she tries to speak, whether from the uphill walk or the fox's attention, she can't say. "You won't believe this fox we just found down in the shed. He came right over and sniffed us. Like a stray cat."

"Really?" says Hutch. In his believing, curious tone, Adeline recognizes a shimmer of the little boy he had been years ago in Cambridge. Or back in September before Thomas left. It stuns her how five short months can transform a boy this age into a nearly unrecognizable creature.

"Whatcha need is a rifle," says Stony from the darkness. "A dead fox is worth fifty bucks easy if you don't screw up its pelt."

"So, can we?" asks Hutch again.

For a moment Adeline forgets about the cookies piled on a platter in the kitchen and thinks that her son is asking permission to murder a fox.

I DO NOT LIKE THE bus. It rattles and that makes my head ache. I can't concentrate with all the shaking and the kids screaming.

Sylvia doesn't have to ride the bus because her mother still picks her up from school. Mama says that I am too mature for that. Plus, Mama says she can't be driving to and fro now like some damned chauffeur. Still, I don't like to sit by myself on a bus that makes me sick, even if it is for only three point two miles. It is better today because Stony sits with me and Hutch sits behind us. Stony wears a winter hat all the time, even today when it is warm and drippy outside, and Hutch didn't even bring a coat to school. Stony makes people laugh. Mrs. Sampson told me to laugh or at least to smile when everyone else does. She showed me the difference between a grimace, a grin, and a smile. We looked at them on her flashcards and I tried to make each face just the way she did, but they all looked the same to me. Teeth. Mrs. Sampson said that I would be as regular as rain when she was done with me. I told her I was already regular because of the prune juice at breakfast and she thought this was funny and she laughed. I laughed, too. She didn't even notice I was doing exactly what she taught me to do. Stony says that he likes my new glasses. He takes them off my face and tries them on and makes a grimace, or maybe a grin, then puts them back on me. He misses and pokes them into my ear and then the glasses feel cockeyed. I don't like that he's touching my face, but instead of telling him to get away, which is what I would say to Hutch, I tell him thank you for the kind compliment. Hutch tells Stony to leave me alone, but Stony says he is just talking to me and what is Hutch's problem? It is true that he is just talking to me, so why does Hutch make a mad face? Then Stony tells me to say a new word he just learned. Dickwad. I want to know what it means and he says just say it. When I do say it, Stony laughs. I say it louder and everybody else laughs, too. Hutch tells me to shut up and calls me a moron. This word I already know because Sylvia explained it to me and I double-checked in Daddy's Oxford English Dictionary to be sure she got it right. Sylvia gets plenty of things wrong. I say the new word again and stick out my tongue at Hutch. When everyone laughs again, I laugh, too, without even having to plan it first.

STONY LIVES IN AN apartment above a gas station with his dad and two older brothers. His mom took off a while ago, but Hutch doesn't know when exactly. Judging from the scum around the place, it was probably years ago now. It isn't the kind of thing Hutch talks about with Stony. He sticks to the mutually agreed topics of *Call of Duty* and *Halo*, with occasional forays into sex and which middle school teacher is the biggest douchebag. Stony is cool. You don't go telling a guy like that about your AWOL dad or your nightmares or the acid swishing around in your guts, unless you want to be called a pussy and demoted to the assholes' table in the cafeteria.

The Stones keep the red floral curtains in their living room drawn all the time to block glare from their enormous flat-screen TV. It's bright outside today, so light seeps through the fabric and makes the whole room feel all blood-and-guts. It's hot in here, too. That clanking radiator must have a busted thermostat since it's a tropical heat wave outside. Still, their TV is awesome and worth the rest of it. At home, there's only the small, ancient TV that Hutch's grandmother used to watch *Jeopardy!* and *CSI* before she had a stroke and died right there on the sofa. Hutch's parents gave the sofa to the Salvation Army but didn't replace it, so now Hutch and Lizzy have to lie on the floor to watch their shows. Hutch's grandfather died in a nursing home before Hutch was old enough to care about what shows the old man liked to watch. He's curious now, but his mother thinks he's just being disrespectful to the dead when he asks. Hutch's dad doesn't believe in television at all, and if it were up to him—he likes to say every time he sees one on—theirs would be up at the dump next Saturday. But his mom likes her occasional program, things set in the olden days or nature documentaries or shows about fixing up your house. She watches them while puttering around trying to look busy. Hutch keeps telling her that there's loads of her kind of stuff on the cable stations, but she can't be swayed to sign up, at least not yet. Another winter without Dad might do the trick.

Hutch stands before the giant screen in the Stones' gory, suffocating room, controller in hand, locked in epic battle. His eyes and hands twitch, and he mumbles to himself. At this moment, he *is* a special-ops sniper taking out as many insurgents with as much bloodshed as possible. He moves fluidly through the enemy's lair, snapping around corners and firing a few clearing rounds before he crosses open windows. He could never sit still while he played these games the way some guys do. Or talk, except in character. Three other boys drape themselves across the furniture, scrounging Cheetos crumbs from the bottom of snack bags they filched from Mr. Stone's convenience mart and licking their fingers clean of the telltale orange residue. The apartment reeks of unleaded fuel. The swimsuit issue of *Sports Illustrated* is splayed on the coffee table where Stony's brothers pick it up whenever they pass through, flipping the worn pages until they wilt.

Hutch's mom won't let him get an Xbox. She won't even let him play any game on the computer involving a gun or blood. Plus, he gets only one hour a day of computer time. Even that's an upgrade, though, from the thirty minutes he got before Dad took off. Mom must have been feeling weak about Dad being such a jerk. Or maybe it was a bribe to get him to back her up on the lies she tells Lizzy. That Santa and the Tooth Fairy are real. That Dad is on a "trip." Hutch isn't above bribery. Still, it hasn't gotten him an Xbox. If he wants to play *Call of Duty* he has to go to Stony's house and then lie to his mother when she asks what they did all afternoon over there. Stony calls Hutch's mother an uptight bitch for not letting Hutch play whatever and whenever he wants, and Hutch doesn't confirm or deny the accusation. When Stony loses to Hutch or is otherwise having a bad day, he asks if Hutch wants to play a little-kid game like *Mario Kart*. Hutch tells him to *shut up, asshole,* which is the conditioned and approved response, but the truth is that *Mario Kart* isn't so bad. At least it doesn't leave him nauseated and wired like the war games do. After he plays those, he can't fall asleep alone in his room. When he closes his eyes, the world comes into electronic focus, jolting and moving as if an invisible controller were in his hand. He tells his mom he feels sick or has a headache so that she will let him curl up with her and Lizzy for a little while. He doesn't mention the shadowy men who pursue him at night. He doesn't confess that his dream-self has done horrific things: severed heads and limbs, reveled in spurting blood, turned his back on his comrades-in-arms. When he wakes, sweat-soaked from running desperately through a war zone looking for someone who can stop his marauding, his mother wants to know what on God's green earth he is dreaming of. *Dad,* he says.

Stony stands next to Hutch.

"I *got* it, Stony," Hutch says.

"Dude, go left. Left." Stony shakes his head when a commando blows Hutch away. "I told you. Give it up, dickwad. My turn."

When it is not his turn, Hutch is instantly bored. The boys on the sofa are such losers. The kind of kids who spend half their days in detention and the other half in remedial English. Stony likes them because they are, he says, *obedient*.

After the other boys go home, Stony asks Hutch who he would rather see naked: Mrs. Sampson or the lady in the cafeteria with the mole by her upper lip. Hutch tells him to shut up. He doesn't waste his time thinking about old ladies.

"Yeah, then who do you think about? Bri-an?" Stony sings out the name and bats his lashes. Brian Lestig is a certifiable flamer. Hutch sometimes meets him on a Sunday—not that he'd ever admit it—to play tennis at the high school courts. It's a sport his dad pushed on him a little too hard, but he likes it anyway.

"Shut up, Stony. Don't be such a douche. At least I'm not jerking off to friggin' *Sports Illustrated* models." Hutch kicks the magazine off the coffee table. "It's pathetic."

"Nah, that's my brothers'. I go for the ones I can see in the flesh. You see the new sub? She is un-fucking-believable."

"No one over twenty-five is hot. It's a proven fact."

"I don't know, dude. Your mom is pretty hot," says Stony.

"Shut up," says Hutch.

"I'm serious, dude. Hot. My dad says she was really uptight in high school. A real waste of a fine piece of ass." Stony laughs and tosses himself onto the sofa. He moans, "Oh, Addy. Baby."

"Go fuck yourself," says Hutch. He wants to jump on top of Stony, knee him in the balls or maybe punch him in the nose or something, but the impulse seems to shrivel up in his brain and not quite make it to his body. He's got nothing. No guts at all without a controller in hand. "You're such an asshole," he says and throws the controller hard at Stony who is now writhing in mock ecstasy on the sofa, thrusting his hips skyward and grunting. Hutch's aim is off. The controller misses Stony's head and knocks a half-empty can of Coke onto the carpet.

"Nice throw, faggot," says Stony, laughing now and rescuing the spilling can.

Hutch can barely pedal his bike back home. He is sweating, and his face is flushed. Stony is such a loser. Hutch could have said something about Stony's mom being a slut who ran away. Ditched him. He could have rubbed that in Stony's face, but he's not a jerk. He has limits. Halfway home, Hutch stops thinking about what he should have done to Stony and starts wondering if it's possible that his mom is hot. She doesn't look like those girls in *Sports Illustrated*. She's too big, for one thing. Pretty, maybe. But hot? Stony might be making fun of him, but Hutch has seen how Stony's dad is way nicer to his mother than to anyone else buying gas. He actually smiles. Once he winked. And he calls her Addy. Since Gramma died, there's no one else who does that. Mr. Stone even gives Lizzy free candy, right from the rack, not just dusty lollipops like the bank hands out, but real Kit Kats and Snickers.

That night, an insurgent stalks Hutch early in his sleep, and he sneaks into bed with Lizzy and Mom before midnight. When he falls back asleep, curled against his mother's back, he is in a dark house, sitting on a sofa—only it's *their* old sofa, plaid and scratchy, the one Gramma died on. Stripes of light bleed through shuttered windows. And Hutch is waiting. Somehow he knows he's supposed to just sit there and not do anything. He doesn't know why he's waiting, but he's nervous. Then the door to the next room opens, and Hutch is suddenly in the doorway. It's his mother. Kneeling on a bed, her head hung low and her face blocked by her hair. Behind her, Mr. Stone's big hands squeeze his mother's ass, shiny in pink satin panties, and then he gives her a not-so-light spank. She throws her head back and groans and laughs. Mr. Stone winks at Hutch and lets loose a wide and toothy grin.

When they get ready for school the next morning, Hutch can't help looking at his mother's breasts, braless beneath her worn-thin white T-shirt, swaying as she brushes her teeth, her nipples thick and dark, unavoidable. Hutch now knows, without doubt, that he is the biggest loser-pervert ever. His stomach twists up at the thought of it. When his mom tousles his hair and tells him to hop in the shower before it gets too late, he slaps her hand away. Surprise flashes in her eyes, and then anger pinches them down just a tiny bit, and he thinks for a moment that she will yell at him—he needs her to yell at him. He's not some baby. He can make up his own mind about when to take a shower; she should leave him alone. He wants to scream this at her. The words are right there, just waiting for her to trigger them. But, instead, she leaves him standing at the sink, toothbrush raised, and says that she'll make him bacon for breakfast, if he wants. Yes, he wants. Of course, he wants. But he says, "No. Forget it. It's donut day."

THE FOX SNATCHED ONE of my Ameraucanas. Number 3. Daddy got her from a farmer he knows. We traded some of our seeds for his chicks. We got twelve Ameraucanas and twelve Rhode Island Reds. One of the Reds died right away and I buried her in our pet-memory place down by the pond even though she is not a pet. I know better than to name any of them. They are livestock. I am their breeder. I was glad it was a Red that died because I like the Ameraucanas better. Some of them lay eggs that are blue like my room and some of them are green like lima beans. I like both, but neither color is as good as the blue of the robin eggs we found last spring in a nest in the holly bushes next to the barn. I did not touch those eggs. Hutch is wrong about that. I did not scare the parents away. The eggs just fell from the nest and broke. Maybe when it was so windy. Maybe a squirrel knocked it over. I still have the broken bits in my treasure drawer. I don't know if the robins will come back to that nest again this year. Mama says no. Robins aren't like that. Hutch says: no way, José, because the birds know that there's a robin murderer in the house. Mama told Hutch to put a cork in it. Daddy winked and said that sure the birds will come back because it was a good nest and robins have a short memory for tragedy. I'm not sure why Daddy winked about this. It didn't seem funny to me. If the robins come back, I won't let the fox get them.

THE THAW GIVES THE farm a drippy sound. Droplets fall from the icicles edging the roof where the ice is a foot thick and translucent spikes dangle like a frozen portcullis. Sheets of snow slide periodically from the sun-baked roof in startling whooshes. Adeline wonders: What determines when an icicle will finally harpoon to the ground, when snow will finally let go of the roof, when a branch will snap in a light breeze after having withstood the two blizzards that blew through in January? All around her, nature is finding this tipping point and trying, greedily, to move from winter to spring. The shoveled paths in the barnyard—from the porch to the coop and down to the woodshed—have melted until now mud appears in patches and the paths feel less like trenches than gentle suggestions of which way to go. But it's an illusion, even after half a week of melt: snow is still high in the farmyard, slushy and slippery to walk on. From beneath the massive snowbanks piled at the end of the driveway by the plow, rivulets of water escape, making their gentle way down the slope from the farm to the road, gathering and twisting into a torrent that carves a gully alongside the driveway deep enough to trap a car tire if you aren't careful. In the afternoon light, the snow's surface turns pale blue, the color of the children's cold lips when they stay out to play longer than they should, but deep below that, there is a hint of warm pink, like a hidden pulse.

The smell of fox around the woodshed has intensified with the long spate of warm weather. Adeline has told Hutch to get going on more mousetraps, but she hasn't seen him take action. She should demand that he listen to her. Consequences are an anchor of her parenting philosophy. But even the possibility of a confrontation leaves Adeline wilted. What power does she really have to enforce anything on Hutch at this point? On the other hand, the fox took one of Lizzy's chickens. He loosened the bottom edge of the mesh in a shade-free spot where the sun could concentrate itself all day and completely melt the snow down to the mud. There's no stopping the fox now that he's unearthed a steady supply of food. All hell will break loose if more chickens are eaten. It's too alarming to consider.

Adeline picks her way around the neat rows of firewood, peering into crevices and using her nose to sniff out the fox's den. There's a hole in the stone foundation that looks suspicious, but his smell is too overwhelming in such a cramped space for her to discern its source for certain. She collects the old mousetraps to bring up to the barn to jumpstart Hutch. She examines Thomas's old Havahart trap that Lizzy set up this morning, baiting it with strips of leftover bacon from breakfast. Lizzy must really want that animal gone to give up her favorite food. Adeline removes the bacon from the trap and drops it by the crevice.

The woodshed feels dangerous to Adeline today, as it has since last fall when the Devil ensnared Thomas there, replacing the man she had known for nearly two decades—the man with big, romantic, change-the-world plans—with someone who doesn't call or write or email, not even on his son's birthday. It has crossed Adeline's mind that maybe something horrible has happened. Maybe Thomas is dead. This actually soothes her a little. It would be less hurtful, wouldn't it? More tragic, but less pathetic. Some days, she thinks this is what she wants. A period at the end of this sentence. But then Adeline receives another check in the mail, the ones that Thomas has commanded some Connecticut lawyer to send to her, drawn from a trust that Adeline didn't know existed, and accompanied by a curt, explanatory note on the lawyer's thick, creamy letterhead. She tries to take this as a good sign. She tries to feel relieved and loved and optimistic.

Thomas used to tell Adeline in the wee hours on an undersized dorm bed that he wanted to make something real out of his life. Their life. He had grown up privileged, calloused more from a tennis racket and an oar than from a shovel and an ax, but he wanted to leave all that behind. There were a few false starts after college and then, finally, on a visit to Adeline's parents one Fourth of July weekend, he got his big idea. He would become a seed farmer. He would raise fruits and vegetables and collect their seeds. The root of everything good. The beginning of life. And as he had envisioned from the porch swing on the back of this very house, the Vermont Seed Company now exists. They sell only organic, heirloom seeds. The same vegetables that Adeline's grandmother once served at dinner. The ones she put in the huge root cellar in endless rows of plenty. Everything Thomas grows is rare and uncorrupted by modern technology. Of course, if enough clever, industrious farmers grew Thomas's vegetables and saved enough seeds for their next crop, they could quickly put Vermont Seed out of business. When Adeline's mother once brought up this gaping hole in Thomas's business plan, he shrugged. *If that happens,* Thomas said after a moment, *then I will have begun a revolution.*

When Thomas taught Hutch to pitch a curve or took Lizzy to the pond at the bottom of their meadow to hang a rope swing, he seemed utterly joyous and at peace in the life he had forged. How Adeline had envied this contentment. She had feigned excitement for the next year's growing plans and made chit-chat with the other privileged do-gooders-turned-farmers that Thomas had befriended, but her restlessness had rattled inside her, a caged thing. How was this life of laundering towels, sweeping pine floors, making endless meals, and praying that the weather cooperated, any different from what earlier generations of her kind had endured? But Adeline had born her dissatisfaction internally, individually, not wanting to sully Thomas's joy.

And then, at the end of last September, Thomas began to split wood with a fervor she hadn't seen since their first season on the farm when she had worried he'd keel over from lack of sleep. They needed the wood. Things had been too busy in the spring to get enough split. It all made sense for a few days. A week even. But when it didn't stop, Adeline suggested that they borrow a splitter to get the job done faster. Thomas scoffed, saying that he found it cathartic, good for the soul, to swing his ax. The weeks turned into a month, and Adeline began to spy on Thomas from the window above the kitchen sink. She watched his endless exertions while she washed and dried the dishes. While she shelled peas and peeled apples. Not once did he divert from his task. His whole face squeezed shut in the effort. Adeline told herself that it was just his way of dealing with the disappointment of the growing season, especially with this year's seed yield being so low. He still had a lot to learn. Five years was just the beginning for a new farmer. He was coming to grips with that. She called her friends back in Cambridge. Midlife crisis, everyone concurred. Adeline tried to accept this explanation. Still, nothing rational could explain it to her satisfaction. Her friends hadn't seen him pounding away with that ax, possessed. His wide-eyed vengeance growing day by day, until sore spots formed on his palms, and the spots became blisters, and the blisters tore, wept, bled and, then, begrudgingly, calloused. Each night Adeline ministered them and respectfully mentioned that surely there was enough wood by now. She ached with both a longing for her husband's attention and a fear of losing him altogether if she made her needs known. The two pains became inextricably interwoven inside her like rows of stockinette stitch: knit, purl, knit, purl.

On a Sunday afternoon, a week before Halloween, Adeline felt a seismic shift in the rhythm of Thomas's obsession. Later she would not be able to describe it. On the surface everything was the same as it had been the previous day, and the days before that. The same chopping and stacking. The same glazed, distant expression. But even as she cleared the lunch dishes and gave Hutch permission to go to the fall fair at school, she knew they were nearing the end of something. She left the kitchen window open, let the too-expensive heat hemorrhage out into the yard, and bribed Lizzy with Chutes and Ladders. Lizzy was too old for the game, but she still loved its clear morality, its gratifying just desserts. For a while, it was enough for Adeline just to hear Thomas working outside and to watch her and Lizzy's little cardboard characters behave well and then poorly. Slowly climbing up. Too fast tumbling back down. The crack of ax against block, the clatter of logs proved that Thomas was right there.

"Now you spin, honey." Adeline tapped her finger on the cardboard spinner. "Lizzy?"

Before she responded, Thomas burst into the house through the back door. He smelled of earth and iron and sweat. Adeline hoped for a moment that he had finally finished the chopping and had come in to reclaim her, but then she saw his clenched face as he powered past her and Lizzy.

"You keep playing, okay?" Adeline said to Lizzy, who was watching the spinner twirl. "I'll be right back."

Thomas snatched jeans and plaid shirts and sneakers from his bureau and stuffed them into a huge army-green duffle bag that used to belong to Adeline's father, just like nearly everything else Thomas and Adeline owned. Thomas emerged from the back of the closet with hangers of dress clothes. These were clothes from another era. From the days after college when he and Adeline had worked for save-the-world agencies and bought furniture at flea markets and played grown-up. Some were from college even. Back when his family had different expectations for him, and he had rebelled by marrying Adeline and becoming a social worker and then, worse yet, moving to a farm in the middle of nowhere.

Adeline followed Thomas around, a needy dog, leaning against doorframes. She followed him onto the porch, twisting up a dish towel in her hands. He could not get to the truck fast enough. "I'll call," he said.

Adeline knew she should ask the expected questions— why? or what? or who? or where? —but nothing came out. Thomas looked at the house one last time, slapped the hood of his truck, and that was that. Adeline was left standing there like the abandoned farmer's wife she was. A farmer's daughter. A farmer's granddaughter. Barely escaped to the ivy-covered quads before Thomas swept her up and brought her back to the start. Like the broken cookie jar in Chutes and Ladders. Adeline listened to the ghost-hum of Thomas's engine a full ten minutes after she lost sight of him. It became more than a sound. Or maybe her ears became more than ears. It was a vibration in the ground itself, stinging her hands like a hammer struck on metal. It filled her with its tinny rattle, making the fair hair that coated her body stand erect and landing with a final, deep resonance in her gut.

When Adeline returned to the coffee table, Lizzy had rearranged the game board, lining up Adeline's cardboard child with all the others: little, smiling soldiers. Lizzy had added rows of miniature plastic animals and tiny Polly Pocket dolls and LEGO men that she kept in a rusted Scooby-Doo lunch box that Adeline had once carried to school.

Over dinner, Adeline told Hutch that his dad was taking a trip, doing some research for the farm. *He'll be here for Halloween*, Lizzy said confidently. *Actually, maybe not*, said Adeline. *How long then? Thanksgiving? Christmas?*

Definitely Christmas, Adeline said. Her explanations were weak and controvertible had Lizzy decided to accurately recount what had happened while she was lining up her battalions of miniatures, but blessedly there were no big lies. Thomas's silence had been a parting gift: the story between now and when he returned—for he *would* return, this she knew—would be Adeline's to tell as she saw fit.

After the children were finally asleep that night, in her and Thomas's bed for the first time in years, Adeline had snuck to the woodshed looking for clues. Surely there would be yellowed newspaper clippings documenting a disturbing obsession, or secret stashes of drugs or booze or porn, or love letters bundled with satin ribbon: the kinds of things that made policemen nod sagely to one another in sanctimonious, communal understanding. It had to be something tremendous that would send Thomas running away from them. Do men really leave because their big plans aren't quite as big as they had hoped? Stupidly, the last thing Adeline had expected to find was cord after cord of perfectly split and stacked wood. She couldn't even enter the shed because the wood came right to the threshold of the double doors. The stacks were tidy and tight, architectural in their layout. It was more than enough to last the winter. He had even split the tarped cords outside the shed. It was enough that it would probably rot before they used it up. Just seeing all that forethought and care made her queasy.

Back in the big barn, Adeline dumps the mousetraps on the counter by the utility sink. She sits on a bench and yanks off her muddy boots. She can still smell the fox, his aroma teasing her. She wants to see him again. Chicken thief or not, there was an otherworldly allure about him. And then, as if her desires had conjuring powers, he is there, trotting through the open barn door, beelining for Adeline. He traces figure eights around her ankles like a hungry stray cat. He scratches his chin against her knee. His tail twitches and quivers in indecision before he hops onto the bench beside her. Adeline sits very still with her hands in her lap and waits. She can hear water dripping from the roofline and also in the utility sink with its broken washer, the two making a false echo, first one, then the other, in an irregular, chasing beat. With each drop, the fox's ears cock. He moves so slowly that, for a few minutes, Adeline can't quite tell if he is moving at all until he places his paw on her thigh. The smell of him is pungent but pleasant, like freshly pressed garlic.

The fox isn't much bigger or heavier than a house cat, and he curls up in her lap like one, too, though he doesn't purr. After a few minutes, Adeline rests her hand on him and feels his vibrating heart, the hum of his muscular body, like high-tension wires. She runs her hand the length of him. His fur is dense and silken and much longer than a cat's. Adeline spreads her hand wide and lets the fur slide through her open fingers. She hasn't felt anything so luxurious in a long time. For years it seems she has touched only rough things: the earth, the vegetables, the raw cottons and woolens, Thomas's wind-chafed skin. Not even her children's hair can come close to this slippery, fluid texture, both having inherited her own coarse black curls. The stroking sends waves of pleasure through Adeline's palm and fingers, up her arms, to her armpits. She feels sweaty. Tingles move down the nape of her neck and count off the knobs of her spine, then curl around her tailbone and release into her crotch and inner thighs. All of her is embarrassingly overheated and electric.

From three miles away, in town, comes the tolling of the afternoon bells from First Parish. Only on the stillest of days do these gentle gongs drift within hearing of the farm. Even before Adeline fully registers the sound, the fox slinks from her lap and disappears across the farmyard.

AMERAUCANA #12 WAS SNATCHED *last night. This morning before school I set out the Havahart trap that Daddy used to try to catch the groundhog under the porch. I put my bacon in the trap for the fox. When I catch it, I am going to make Mama drive me fifty miles away so that it won't come back for the rest of my chickens. Mama says it is not the fox that got Ameraucana #3 or #12. She says it was a coyote or maybe the coon hounds that the Stevensons have, the ones that howl all day and night until they get fed. Mama is wrong. I tell her this. I tell her, too, that we still have to get rid of the fox because it is a proven fact that foxes carry rabies. A jogger in Arizona was bitten by a rabid fox and ran for a full mile with it attached to her arm by its teeth. Stony and Hutch are not on the bus today. I saw them riding their bikes out of town while we were waiting for everyone to get on and a kindergartener was late. We have not passed them yet so I think they will beat me home.*

Hutch came with me to the woodshed this morning to set up the trap. He has not met the fox yet. He doesn't believe that it really is tame like Mama said. He wanted to see for himself, but it didn't show.

ADELINE DECIDES TO SHOWER to wash away the raw, buzzing feeling that the fox has stirred in her. The shower water holds the vague smell of swamp and iron that come when the filter for the well needs changing, and Adeline feels a film of this rank water clinging to her. Then the drops of water grow thicker, gaining in momentum and solidity, striking her breasts and face and belly like the first pregnant drops of a spring rain, impossibly big and succulent.

Afterward, Adeline picks up the top pair of utilitarian underwear in her dresser drawer and fingers the graying cotton, softened by endless rounds through the washer, the elastic edging starting to shed its core. She tosses the underpants into the trash can beneath the bathroom sink. In the bottom of the drawer she unearths a pair of black satin panties edged with stiff lace. She bought them last year for Valentine's Day, part of a sexy ensemble that the salesgirl at the mall declared irresistible. Adeline had been desperate to pull a distracted Thomas away from the midwinter anxiety of planning for the spring planting season, from the books and catalogs he perused night after night until their pages tore free from their cheap bindings. Thomas hadn't commented on the outfit even when Adeline wore it once a week until Easter. After that, she got tired of hand-washing it. Bypassed in her dresser drawer day after day, the panties slowly settled like silt to the bottom.

Adeline runs her hand over her ass now, enjoying the smoothness of satin on skin and imagining how it had felt to Thomas whether he acknowledged it or not. She isn't a skinny woman, big-boned her mother once called her, but her body seems immutable regardless of what she eats or whether she exercises. Reliable, she thinks with satisfaction.

Adeline is hunting in her dresser for the matching bra when a sound startles her. Hutch is in the open door frame, the smell of cafeteria, diesel, and wet wool wafting off of him. His eyes slide from Adeline's wet hair to her naked breasts to her black satin crotch, where they stop.

"Hutch!" Adeline says. "Jesus. What do you think you're doing?"

"We just got home," he says, and Adeline realizes that in the shadow of the upstairs hallway lurks Stony. She crosses her arms over her breasts.

Hutch steals a look over his shoulder toward Stony who gives a little snort.

"Get out of here," says Adeline.

Hutch turns without a word and drags Stony by the sleeve toward the stairs. The boys' untied sneakers slap on their way out.

Adeline shoves her bedroom door closed. From the window, she watches the boys pedal down the slick, thawing driveway, their undersized BMX bikes flopping from side to side with their ferocious pumping.

THE RIFLE IS HEAVIER than Hutch had imagined. Stony has taken it out of a closet in his dad's bedroom where it lives next to camouflage pants and Day-Glo safety vests. Mr. Stone's room reeks of old cigarettes and grease. The pillow on his unmade bed still holds a shadowy imprint from the night before. Stony sights with the rifle, like he has spotted a deer in the olive-green plaid curtains.

Stony brags that he can shoot tin cans from thirty yards, and Hutch is impressed though he says that it's no big whoop. He says his dad used to have him take out rabbits and woodchucks that were ruining their crop. Truth was, his dad didn't ever use a gun. Once, a couple of years ago, Hutch's dad had taken him to a shooting range and had some tattooed guy teach them how to use a rifle without killing anybody by mistake. His dad acted like it was some big indoctrination into manhood, those few rounds he let Hutch shoot. Hell, you got more practice with BBs at the YMCA camp. Still, Hutch knows just enough details to go heavy in his tall tale: how many animals he has shot—he measures in dozens—from how far away and how his victims—the kind of critters that his father tried in vain to catch in a Havahart trap—how they splattered on impact.

"What kind of gun does he have?" Stony wants to know.

"Oh, it's like this," Hutch says with false confidence. Their gun was smaller. Or maybe it was Hutch who had been smaller then.

"Yeah? You used *this* for woodchucks?"

"Yeah. I guess. It's been a while."

"Why don't we go out to the dump and shoot some shit?" Stony hands Hutch a box of cartridges.

"Now?"

"Yeah."

"I don't know, man. It's kind of late. It's gonna get dark."

"Yeah, I guess. Maybe tomorrow." Stony grabs a cigarette from the pack on his father's nightstand and offers one to Hutch, who waves him off. Only once has Hutch smoked a cigarette with Stony. His mom had sniffed it on him like a bloodhound as soon as he walked in the door and grounded him for the rest of the week.

Stony says, "Next time you talk to your dad, ask him what kind of gun he's got." The unlit cigarette bounces up and down in his lips and slurs his words.

"Sure, sure," says Hutch.

"Hey, we're picking up my .22 this weekend."

"Cool."

"You still got that fox in your shed? I was thinking we could break in my rifle on it."

"Oh, I don't know. My mom wouldn't want us shooting on the farm."

"It's doing your mom a favor. Didn't she want to get rid of it? Besides, who says she needs to know? I'll even split the money with you if we don't fuck up the pelt. Fifty-fifty."

"I don't know, dude. I'd get in deep shit if she found out." Hutch hopes the swear word will make him sound less afraid.

Stony juts out a hip into his version of a womanly pose and says, "*Now, Hutchinson, honey, did you set out those mousey traps like a good little boy?*"

"Shut up."

"Jesus, you do everything your mother says, don't you?"

"No, but—"

"You said your dad let you shoot, right? Didn't your mom know about that?"

"That's different. My dad was there and—"

"And now he's not."

"Shut up, Stony."

"I'm just saying, if your dad's gone AWOL, I don't see why you don't step up. You know what I'm saying?"

Stony puts his dad's rifle back in the closet.

Lying had never worked that well for Hutch. He watched other kids like Stony do it all the time, as automatically as scratching an itch. But Hutch's lies made his body flush and his eyes flit and his words stammer. The more he lies the deeper the panic sets in. He wants to go home now. He says, "I haven't shot anything in a while. I'd probably just miss."

"What about all those fucking woodchucks?"

"Woodchucks are slower than foxes. And fatter."

"Isn't the fucker tame, anyway?"

"I don't know. I haven't seen it." Hutch has been wondering if the fox is tame for real. He's checked for it with Lizzy and on his own and has never even spotted it. But his mother claims it followed her into the barn and let her pet it. That it's too tame to even know how to kill chickens. It's possible, probable even, that it's one of those bullshit things his mom makes up for Lizzy because it sounds like magic. Because maybe then Lizzy won't obsess over getting rid of it.

"C'mon," says Stony. "It'll be awesome. Even your dumbass sister couldn't miss a tame fox."

ADELINE CURLS ON HER side and moves her fingers noiselessly between her legs while Lizzy sleeps soundly beside her. She does her best not to pant. She pinches her eyes closed and rubs a little faster, squeezing tight every muscle between her thighs and her stomach. Twice she has come close to climaxing only to become distracted at the crucial moment: by the house's settling creaks, by Lizzy's congested snuffles, by the sound of dripping on her window ledge. She redirects her mind to the task at hand, searching for a suitable fantasy, but all that comes are thoughts of Thomas, or, Lord help her, Lance Stone, or, worst of all, one of Stone's sons. One of the older ones. Not Stony. Definitely not. But none of these potential suitors brings her where she wants to go. Her mind drifts back to the fox as though by magnetism. She pushes aside the thought of his delicate tongue on her skin, though it causes a vibration in her crotch and her fingers twitch faster despite herself. With her free hand she gently squeezes her nipple until it goes rigid. Her concentration is complete. A wave moves through her and she is nearly there, until it ebbs again without crashing. She pauses to catch her breath, frustrated and raw.

"Mom?"

Adeline's eyes open and there is Hutch in the shadows in only his gray briefs despite the old-house chill.

"Jesus, Hutch. You scared me."

"I'm sorry."

"No, no. It's okay." Adeline sits up and does her best to seem sleepy. "I was just dozing off." She can make out the musky smell of her deepest self on her fingertips. She buries them beneath the covers, compressed under her thigh.

"I can't sleep."

"Hmm."

"I've tried reading."

"Just close your eyes and rest. Don't try so hard."

Hutch sits down on the edge of her bed, the same way Adeline used to when she tucked him in at night. It is impossible to remember the last time she pulled up his quilt, kissed his forehead, and switched off his light. When was the last time Adeline had cut off his crusts, or tied his shoes, or brushed his hair?

Feet still anchored to the floor, Hutch tips over and lays his torso down on the bed. Adeline sinks back, too. They both face the edge, his back to her front, spoons in a drawer. He is on top of the covers; she is buried beneath. Adeline kisses the back of his skull, but then retreats: his hair stinks of oil and sweat.

"Stony got a rifle for his birthday. It's a Marlin .22." Hutch's voice is low and wistful. He pulls his bare feet onto the bed and curls up tighter.

"Since when did you want a gun?" says Adeline.

"I'm just saying *he* got one. Geez."

"I mean if your grandpa were still alive and you wanted to go out with him some time, that'd be okay, but there's no way I'm letting you out of my sight with those Stones on some hunting trip, so don't get any bright ideas about that."

"I didn't even ask. God, Mom, don't freak out."

"And your father would be furious to even hear you talking about it. You only shoot when you have to. Absolute necessity."

"Yeah?" says Hutch, his voice rising in intensity to match her own. "Well, I guess I'll have to ask Dad about that when he comes home."

It is moments like this that test your mettle as a parent, Adeline thinks. She resists the bait. Her restraint is exhausting.

From downstairs comes the sound of the mantel clock striking eleven. Adeline only notices how loud it is when she should be sleeping.

"Time to head back to your own bed, honey."

"When *is* Dad coming home?"

"Oh, Hutch. I told you. Maybe next month. Or in time to plant."

"Really?" He rolls over and looks at her then, desperation in his face.

"Actually, I don't know exactly." When his body tenses, she adds, "He'll be home in spring. Don't worry."

Hutch stays clenched. "It's spring now."

"You know this isn't real."

Adeline pulls her hand out from the covers and rubs Hutch's exposed arm and hip and goose-pimpled thigh before she remembers the smell on her fingers and tucks it away again. Adeline won't be able to relax until she washes her hands.

Their breathing aligns into a steady pulse.

"Can I sleep here tonight?" Hutch says.

"C'mon, honey. You're getting too old for that. I bet Stony doesn't sleep with his dad."

He curls a little tighter like a hedgehog, and pulls the afghan from the foot of the bed over his near-naked body. A single gong for the quarter hour comes from downstairs.

"Okay, time to go," Adeline says.

Hutch stands, but takes no steps toward the door.

Into the dark, Adeline says, "I'll take you guys to get donuts in the morning. How's that?"

"All right," he says, and Adeline can just make out his shrug through the blackness.

MY TRAP IS STILL *empty. The bacon keeps disappearing. The fox is too tricky for me. I told Mama that what I need to use is a spring trap. Or live bait. We could get a mouse at Pet Circle and somehow put it in the Havahart. When we were in Vanderhof's Hardware on Saturday, I saw a spring trap that would work. Mama says this is cruel and what am I thinking. But it is more cruel to let my Ameraucanas be eaten. I have tried to be humane but now I must use a better tactic. Daddy taught me all about tactics when we played chess. They force your opponent's hand. Limit their options. Like I need to limit the fox's options. Hutch laughs when I talk about my plan at dinner and says, fat chance. Mama tells him to stop. But I say that there is a fat chance. A very fat chance. That fox will not get one more of my Ameraucanas. I have money saved up from Grandmother and Grandpapa from my birthday. I just need to borrow ten dollars from Mama. Grandmother and Grandpapa didn't send any money this Christmas, otherwise I would have enough to buy the spring trap without having to make a deal with anyone. Hutch says they didn't send us Christmas money because Daddy isn't here, but they never sent money to Daddy anyway, so I don't see what difference it makes if he is on a trip or not. I want to call him because I want to get more Ameraucanas from that man he knows. I don't want to lose my chance. But Mama says Daddy's too busy for any calls right now. She says the same thing whenever I ask to call Daddy. Busy doing what? Her forehead pinches up when I say that. Then she says that Daddy's busy with grown-up work and I shouldn't bother him with my stupid chickens, only she doesn't use the word* stupid. *Hutch's milk squirts out his nose when she uses the word that isn't* stupid— *I'm not supposed to say it, so I won't. Mama sends him to his room, which seems unfair since she used the word and not him. Hutch makes chicken bawks and flaps his wings and chicken dances while he walks to the stairs. Mama tells him he can't play on the computer for the rest of the week. Who cares, he says, but he does care, so I don't know why he says that. Mama yells up the stairs that she has had quite enough of Hutch's stuff. She doesn't use the word* stuff *either. When she comes back to the table, I ask again why we can't call Daddy about the Ameraucanas man. Mama puts her head on the table.*

THE FOX IS EAGER and trips past Adeline into the kitchen. It has been easy to get him into the house. At first, Adeline had to lure him out of the woodshed with leftover breakfast bacon, but after that he hadn't required any coaxing at all. Now he's following her around in her daily routine of dishes and laundry and vacuuming, even the noise of that old Hoover doesn't scare him away. The fox is entirely remarkable and, yet, feels astoundingly normal. There are things far stranger than a tame fox. Some of which have happened to Adeline.

By midafternoon, the chores done, Adeline sits on her bed and waits. She has done this every day this winter when the kids are at school. She tells herself that she is resting or meditating or planning, but it is waiting. Plain and simple. But for what? The fox hops onto the bed and curls up in Adeline's lap to wait with her. She keeps thinking of him as a cat, keeps waiting for him to purr when she strokes his orange fur. Maybe she has been waiting for him, she thinks.

Adeline stares out the window at the gray expanse of the farmyard with its melting paths and, beyond that, the flat whiteness of the back meadow, still snow-shrouded despite more than a week of warm temperatures. Her eyes trace the ancient stone walls that divvy up the land as if they were a maze with an exit she will find if she just concentrates hard enough. It's a game she has played since childhood.

Adeline gently pulls the fox to her chest while she maneuvers herself into a comfortable position for a nap. She wriggles awkwardly out of her jeans, covers her feet and legs with the afghan—the last one that her grandmother had crocheted—and props her head on two pillows. How many times has she made these same motions with a baby in her arms, careful to keep him sleeping so she could nap herself?

Adeline, warm beneath the fox and the afghan, dreams of water spinning down drains, washing away mud and blood from her hands. Then she dreams of treacherous eddies in Black Creek, the kind that drowned her uncle when he was just a teenager. Everywhere in her dreams is the sound of trickling water, as if not only the filthy snow piles and the lumpy icicles were melting, but also the ground itself, the stones in their century-old walls, the split rail fences that once kept cows in and town boys out. All of it is melting, a drop at a time, overheated by a series of sixty-degree days. The farm is disintegrating like ice in hot tea. She dreams of her mother's prized white chintz sofa floating free in the parlor, Thomas's great dictionary washing down the basement stairs. The water rises at tsunami speed from the pond at the bottom of the meadow and from the creek that feeds it and from their well and from the melting snow and from the slipping ice until the farm is deluged and the only survivor is Adeline. She fears that she too will wash away and then there will be no one left to meet the children when they step off the bus.

The fox jolts Adeline awake by licking the remnants of bacon grease from her hand. It is a scent that only the fox and Adeline can smell. His licks are tender and purposeful like a mother lion cleaning her cub. He moves slowly up the back of Adeline's wrist where it rests across her exposed belly, tickling her until the hairs on her body stand erect. She lies utterly still. The fox continues to lick now at her navel until something forbidden flutters inside Adeline and her nipples stiffen in the over-warm room. She shifts her weight and slides the afghan down a fraction, exposing the edge of her underwear. She runs her fingertip back and forth along the elasticized edge while the fox works diligently on her abdomen. She tightens her innermost core in little pulses. Then, as abruptly as he began, the fox stops. He lifts his heads and listens. He hops off the bed and trips out of the room, leaving Adeline full of ache, the still-moist and exposed parts of herself chilling in the air.

Adeline buries her face in her hands and steeps in the sweet, safe smell of fox.

HUTCH LIES ON HIS bed and turns up his music and wonders how it is possible that he went along with Stony's game. They were supposed to be keeping an eye on the girls, Lizzy and her little friend. Sylvia is her name. *Just let them watch TV*, his mom had said. *Mrs. Sampson won't stop bugging me until I go down there. No computer, Hutch. I mean it.* The girls had on some dumb rerun. Stony and Hutch were a few feet away at the kitchen table, each on a bench. Stony kept complaining that it sucked being at Hutch's house. There's nothing good to do. Hutch was a pussy for following his mom's rules.

Hutch had felt itchy under his skin to suggest something good. He spun the salt and pepper shakers. He needed something Stony-worthy, but all he could come up with was listening to music or eating snacks and both sounded lame.

"Hey, why don't we play a game?" said Stony. "You got some cards?"

"Yeah, sure." Hutch had been so relieved. He found a deck of cards in the junk drawer in the kitchen. He counted them out to fifty-two. Even that ate up a few minutes. "What games do you know?"

Stony said, "I was thinking poker. You know Texas Hold 'Em?"

"No," said Hutch, a flush rising on his neck. He didn't know any gambling games. He tried to save face by shuffling the cards like a pro, something he had learned from his grandmother during his first winter on the farm. "You know cribbage?"

Stony looked at Hutch like he had suggested Go Fish and then said, "Blackjack's easy. I'll teach you. It'll be better with more players."

The boys looked over at the TV and the girls lying on the rag rug. Hutch said, "Lizzy, you guys wanna play cards?"

Lizzy and Sylvia gave each other smiles of concurrence and quick nods, like they had been sitting there just hoping against hope that the boys would want to play with them. Hutch figured they were just as bored of grainy reruns as he was. They tried blackjack but Sylvia wasn't good at games and kept screeching, "Hit me!" before collapsing into a giggling heap. So they switched to Old Maid because everybody already knew it. Hutch can't remember just how long they played before they all started to get bored, and then Stony suggested that they bet money for each hand. He took a wad of ones and some coins out of his pockets. The money sat there on the table, and Hutch couldn't quite see the angle Stony was going for. Hutch didn't want to lose what little money he had to Stony by playing cards with the girls, and the girls didn't have any money anyway. The girls started building little pyramids with the cards while Hutch and Stony debated. Then Stony said he had an idea. They could play the way his brothers did: loser has to take off a piece of clothing. The girls laughed and looked at each other and laughed again. Hutch and Stony laughed. Hutch wasn't sure if Stony was serious, but then he started shuffling and giving the rules. Each sock would count as an item. No adding extra layers. It was all a big joke. Strip poker with little girls. Not that they called it that. It wasn't that. Not really. Everyone kept giggling, and Stony winked at Hutch. Hutch couldn't believe the girls would do it. But they did. It was hilarious for a little while. The girls lost most of the time, of course. Stony was the dealer. And they dutifully took off their socks, one at a time, and their headbands and T-shirts. They hunched low to hide their nakedness beneath the edge of the kitchen table. Hutch took off only his belt and one sock. When the girls had no clothes left, Stony made them do jumping jacks or cartwheels or sprints across the room to pay for their losing hands. And then, as if he had scripted it all along, when the clock struck five, he collected his coat, told the girls that it had been real, and pedaled off. The girls pulled their clothes back on and sat back down in front of the TV as if the intervening hour hadn't happened. Hutch put the cards away and made microwave popcorn for Sylvia and Lizzy before his mom came home. He thought about reminding them that this needed to be their little secret. But the more he thought about it, that seemed worse than saying nothing at all.

No harm, no foul, Hutch keeps telling himself. Just a big joke. Nobody got hurt. Everybody had a laugh. The girls didn't have to do it. They could have quit whenever they wanted. And somehow it really *had* been hilarious.

LIZZY RESISTS BATHS AND Adeline has let it slide for nearly a week. But today Lizzy got into chicken shit in the henhouse and its smell clings to her very pores. Mrs. Sampson will probably complain about that next. She'll call home to figure out why Adeline hasn't bathed the child, for God's sake. Mrs. Sampson likes to remind Adeline that kids will find any excuse to tease. Any excuse. *Let's not give them any, okay?* So Adeline draws the bath and coerces Lizzy into it. She washes her hair, hushing the girl when Adeline's hand hits the inevitable nests of tangles. *I am being gentle,* Adeline says.

"Did you see the fox today, Mama? My bacon was gone again."

"No, I wasn't in the woodshed today."

"But the door was closed, and I left it open this morning. I'm sure I did."

Adeline shrugs. Memory isn't perfect. For most people, at least.

The fox has been on Adeline's mind for days. What had really happened in her bedroom? She has sought out the creature in the woodshed, leaving leftover meat, stealing Lizzy's bacon from the Havahart, but so far he hasn't returned for her. It is some kind of omen, Adeline is certain of that, but whether it is a good one or a bad one, she can't decide.

When she piles Lizzy's hair on top of her head in a crazy, sudsy bun, Lizzy says, "So can I get a spring trap?"

"We'll see," says Adeline absentmindedly.

"Tomorrow?"

"What tomorrow?"

"Vanderhof's. For the spring trap. To kill the fox."

"What? No. Jesus, Lizzy, we are not killing that fox."

"If we don't kill it, it will eat all my chickens. And you didn't let me call Daddy. And he doesn't ever call us. Not ever. And what if the Ameraucana man doesn't have any more chicks by the time Daddy gets home from his trip?" Lizzy stands up in the bathtub now, dancing in frustration. Water runs off her, dripping from her fingertips. In that light, with the water on her, Adeline catches a glimpse of budding beneath her daughter's rosy nipples and the jutting of her little hipbones. It seems impossible that this is coming so soon. She is four years younger than Hutch and even he hasn't fully succumbed to puberty yet, his voice still dulcet most of the time. Adeline grabs Lizzy by the elbow to keep her from slipping in the tall porcelain tub.

"Stop hurting me," Lizzy yells and then lets rip a high-pitched shriek.

"I am *not* hurting you. Stop it. Right now." Adeline's grip tightens on Lizzy's elbow, but the dancing and the shrieking only intensify.

"Lizzy, calm down."

Lizzy flaps her loose hand, hitting against Adeline's face and shoulders and neck in her panic.

"Goddamn it, Lizzy. Shut. Up."

When she doesn't, Adeline drags the slippery eighty pounds of girl up and over the edge of the tub and deposits her, still screaming and dripping and wild, onto the bath mat.

THE RIFLE'S REPORT RIPS through the premature singsong of robins, leaving behind a vacant silence. Hutch and Stony are lying on the sun-drenched back porch, all the snow having melted away there. Their legs are splayed and the rifle is propped on an overturned plant pot. It pokes through the railing, aimed at soda and soup cans the boys found in the recycling bin in the big barn and set up on a stone wall at the edge of the barnyard. Lizzy sits on the porch swing, knees drawn up, her chin resting on her kneecaps. She hadn't wanted to watch their target practice, but Hutch had insisted. He didn't trust her not to wander off to her chicken coop or somewhere and end up right in front of a .22 caliber rifle. She was his responsibility, or so his mom liked to say.

"That sucked," says Stony. "You missed by a mile. Give it to me."

He fires the rifle and this time a can cartwheels in the air and rattles to a stop on the crusty ground. Stony grins. "Told ya."

Hutch's hands are shaky. He fires another shot and misses again. "Guess I'm kind of rusty."

"Yeah, I guess so," says Stony.

Hutch's mom could be back any minute. And what if the Stevensons tell her about hearing shots? So what that it's small-game season? Hutch sits up on his knees. "You hungry?" he asks.

"Nah," says Stony. "Hey, Lizzy, you gonna show me this fox of yours or what?" He squints into the shadows where Lizzy is lurking.

"He won't come out for you," says Lizzy. "You smell like that gun."

"Try me. Animals like me."

Hutch eyes the cans again through the rifle sight. If he could settle into his *Call of Duty* zone, if he could channel his inner commando, he could do this.

Then Stony interrupts his concentration. "Lizzy, c'mon. Show me. How am I gonna shoot the fucker for you unless I know where he hides?"

"Okay. Fine," says Lizzy. "But when are you gonna shoot him? He got Rhode Island Red #8 last night."

Stony says, "I'll shoot him today if you can find him for me."

Hutch thinks maybe he should follow them to the shed. Better to be safe. But with each careful shot, his breathing deepens. He becomes a sniper. He blocks his mind. He stops thinking about Stony and Lizzy down in the shed. He stops seeing Stony's smirk when Lizzy and Sylvia jitterbugged naked around the family room. Now there is only the rifle and the target, the squeeze, the crack, and the recoil. He misses again and again, then reloads with another magazine. He stops listening with one ear for his mom's car or Lizzy calling him. His brain rings from the concussive power of the shots. Hutch misses enough times that he loses count and then, miraculously, he connects, sending a Campbell's soup can blasting off the stone wall. He walks over to his aluminum kill and fingers the small entry hole—in and out— where the shot has punctured the can, neatly centered on the word *noodle*.

"Hey," he hollers. No response comes from the woodshed. "Hey, guys," he yells again. "I hit it," he says then into the silence, mostly to himself.

Their mother is at another parent conference with Mrs. Sampson because the teacher won't stop calling. Hutch had picked up the extra phone and listened, worried that Old Maid might come up. Or guns. Or something about the woodshed. But Mrs. Sampson just said *withdrawn* and *distracted* and *chickens*. His mom said she seems just the usual Lizzy to her. Maybe it's the weird weather. Mrs. Sampson must have said *concerned* about six times after that. *Fine,* his mom had said, *fine.*

Hutch presents Lizzy with a plate of her favorite Chips Ahoy and hot chocolate with extra whipped cream.

"C'mon. Take it."

Lizzy dunks one cookie in the drink and slurps it into her mouth. She doesn't take her eyes off the TV. She had hardly spoken to Hutch in a week, not even when he sat next to her in the very first row on the bus and offered up his last stick of gum.

When Stony got on the bus a minute later, he said to Hutch, "I don't wanna sit up here in the fucking nursery school. C'mon back."

Lizzy had pulled her knees to her chest and wrapped her arms around them. She mumbled something into her kneecaps. Hutch thought it might have been "Go away. Please." But whether she was talking to him or Stony he couldn't be sure.

"C'mon. Leave her up here," said Stony. And Hutch had.

HE SITS NEXT TO Lizzy now on the floor and pretends to watch *SpongeBob* for a few minutes. At the commercial, he says, "So. Listen. I've been thinking. About that fox. I've got an idea."

Lizzy eats another cookie. Hutch watches her little hands, her boney wrists decorated with the friendship bracelets she makes for both her and Sylvia, since Sylvia isn't good at that sort of thing. They were the only things the girls hadn't taken off when they played cards. Stony had insisted but the girls said no way. They wouldn't cut them, and that was the only way to take them off, so Stony had to let it go.

"Look, Lizzy, forget about Stony. We don't need him to shoot some stupid fox. I can kill him. We don't need a gun or a spring trap. There's a huge box of mouse bait in the barn. I'll take care of it. Your chickens will be fine. And Mom won't have to know about it. Everything will be okay. I promise."

Lizzy doesn't take her eyes from the screen. She says, almost like a mantra, "Stony is not a good person. I will not play with him again. Not ever."

Hutch's heart pushes against his ribs. He wants to ask Lizzy what has happened, but even the question might conjure the memory of his own barely concealed wickedness.

"I'll do it now, Lizzy. Right now. You wanna come?"

Lizzy shakes her head and doesn't look at Hutch. So he goes alone to make amends. He mixes some of the raw hamburger he is supposed to be making into patties for dinner with mouse bait. He puts the biggest poison meatball inside the crevice where his mother said the fox must have its den. He hides more in chinks in the log wall. He puts them along the foundation where his mother won't notice them if she happens to come down. It'll be like candy for the fox. Candy. Not a bad way to go. And while Hutch works, he talks to the fox that he has never seen. He tells it he is going to get its chicken-eating ass. His hands are gummy with the raw meat. He cleans them on his jeans, and wipes his dripping nose and wet eyes on the sleeve of his sweatshirt. No one messes with Lizzy's chickens. No one.

THE FOX IS HEAVIER dead than Adeline remembers from the moments she held him alive. It is an illusion, maybe, of the airiness of his tail and his lithe, contortionist's body, but dead she can tell he weighs ten pounds easy.

Hutch had announced the fox's death over breakfast that morning.

"Hey, Lizzy," he said. "You won't have to worry about that fox anymore."

Lizzy didn't look up from her bowl of cereal where she was corralling one rogue Cheerio after another with her spoon.

"What?" Adeline asked. Inside her gut something contracted.

"It's dead," said Hutch. "Lizzy, you hear that?"

Adeline's body flushed and she worked to keep her voice level. "What happened?" she asked.

"Beats me. I was just checking the traps this morning and it was dead." Hutch lolled his tongue out of his mouth and rolled his eyes back in his skull in a comedic performance for his sister. "Maybe rabies?"

"Cut it out," said Adeline. She searched his face for signs of secret knowledge. "It just seems pretty strange to me. He was fine on Monday."

"Well, not anymore." Hutch stuck a chunk of melon into his mouth.

Lizzy just kept stirring her milk.

"Lizzy? You hear me?" Hutch asked.

"That Stone boy shot him, didn't he?" Adeline said.

"What? Geez, no. God, Mom."

"I never trusted that boy. I told Dad that he was no good."

Lizzy clenched the edge of the table and jittered her legs up and down, more and more urgently until the table started to vibrate.

Hutch said, "I told you: Stony didn't do anything."

Adeline saw Hutch scan across the table to Lizzy, who shut her eyes in response.

"Keep still, for God's sake," said Adeline. She looked at Hutch, "Where did you put him?"

"At the top of the meadow. I thought you'd be glad to get rid of it."

"By the stone wall or in the pines?"

"I don't know. What difference does it make?" said Hutch. "We gotta go, Lizzy. The bus is gonna be here in two minutes. Get your bag."

As soon as the bus pulled out, Adeline followed Hutch's tracks to find the carcass in a small stand of pines. The fox looked more vulnerable than he had in the woodshed or in her lap or when he caressed her open palm or licked her salty skin. His head was twisted at a funny angle, the underside of his chin facing upward. She nudged him gently, expecting something stiff, but finding him supple. Rigor mortis must have come and gone. He almost looked asleep except for the smell. It wasn't the musk that Adeline had come to love, but the stench of deterioration already beginning. The sweet-sour smell of rot that would summon all the scavenging critters: large, small, and microbial. They would all take their fair share.

Adeline had needed to see him one more time. To be sure that what Hutch said was the whole truth. To know for certain that he would never traipse through their house again. It seemed impossible that her fox had become nothing more than another carcass. How could something so ethereal become so horribly mortal? In those moments with the fox, Adeline had felt herself being pulled skyward and now here they were, in the woods, just a worn-out mother and a dead animal.

She stands now among the lank pines, considering what to do. The place is peaceful enough, with a rolling view down to the pond, but the trees have no sheltering branches, just a few emaciated limbs a ladder's height up. There isn't even any wild brush to hide the poor creature under. Just bare land, the trunks of the pines, and a collapsed stone wall. Adeline breathes through her mouth, avoiding the death smell. She decides to carry the fox to the stand of birches near the pond, to the place her father used to bury his retrievers.

Walking down the meadow is harder than Adeline expected. The temperature finally dropped overnight and the surface of the snow has turned slick. There's a layer of new ice over the softened slush from the thaw. Even with two weeks of warm weather, the snow is still more than a foot deep. God, it has been a long winter. Adeline drops through the ice crust and sinks into snow up to her knee. It sneaks up her pajama pant leg and threatens to steal her boot. It is like walking in frigid mud. She should have worn snowshoes. Keeping the fox balanced in her arms makes everything more difficult. She should have put him in a sack or a carton. She wants to cradle him, but his smell is repugnant, so she holds him at arms' length instead. Adeline sweats. She punches her footsteps across the wide expanse of meadow, stopping several times to rest and unzip or unwrap another layer. Sweat gathers in her crotch and her armpits, damp and then chilled when air penetrates her flannel pajama bottoms. She should have put on jeans. Tears flow from her eyes, and she can't spare a hand to wipe them away.

Adeline tucks the fox under a blueberry bush by the pond. His little body, ruddy against the snow, is a tight ball of orange fur, like a woolly bear caterpillar. He is still beautiful. The color of barley in the setting sun. Adeline thinks about covering him with leaves or branches or some of the crusty snow, but what is the point, really? Any animal hungry enough to eat a dead fox will sniff it out. Besides, being disinterred from a shallow grave seems entirely worse than just rotting away on the surface. Adeline gently repositions the fox's body until she is satisfied that he looks asleep and peaceful. She runs her hand down the long curve of him and resists the bolus of heartache that has lodged in her throat.

She refuses to feel even one iota of pity or pain. She hears her father and grandfather's collective voice reminding her that this is a fox. Better dead than eating Lizzy's hens. Of course. Much better. She was, after all, born a farmer with an inherited understanding of the hierarchy of life. But even so, a tender part of Adeline gives thanks that the fox hadn't been shot. There was that mercy, thank God. Adeline had assumed that her wrath rightly should be aimed at Lance Stone's boy. Why else would Hutch have been so quick to dispose of the carcass? But she had been wrong. Too quick to judge, just like Thomas always said. Maybe she was becoming paranoid. There was no sign of violence. No blood. There was no one to blame, no matter how hard she tried.

Adeline thinks of the children, at school by now. Hutch jostling his locker open, bantering with Stony. She tries to shake away the shadow of dislike that attaches itself to every thought of that boy. And there's Lizzy, tucked into a corner with little wilting Sylvia. Mrs. Sampson and all her *concern*. It's as if she wants there to be some sinister truth beyond the obvious. Why wouldn't a child whose father has left not seem traumatized? Adeline has not thought of her children this carefully these last weeks, and now maternal responsibility pounds back over her like surf. Surely, they are resilient, Adeline thinks. They will be okay. They *are* okay. No matter what Thomas does. Or doesn't do. No matter her own failings. Real spring will come in due course. She's been deluded this one time—distracted—but not again. Maybe she let her guard down a little, but what mother doesn't now and then? No lasting harm done. Right? Adeline stands tall and considers the house at the top of the meadow. Her house. It sits up there, waiting for Adeline to return, to take her in, to shelter her and the children just as it's sheltered those who came before her, insulating them against the dangers of the world. Today the air comes from Canada and carries the smell of ice. It should this time of year. Adeline breathes deep and fills her lungs with its clarifying chill.

El Cenote

The casita gives no room to hide. Not even a bathroom. The tile floor, coated with sand, harbors tiny, biting fleas. There's no ceiling, just the underside of red-clay roof tiles that certainly will leak if it ever bothers to rain. The furniture was roughly hewn by someone who has yet to master the wonders of measurement. The chairs and table teeter on their mismatched legs, threatening to overturn the lit kerosene lamp. Pearls of sap ooze from the cheap pine and stick to my calves. The mosquito netting over the bed is laughable, and a rusted barrel for collecting whatever rain does manage to fall clearly hasn't seen much action lately. Empty five-gallon plastic jugs are piled by the door. My sister, Rita, lugs them home from the boutique resort where she and her boyfriend work. Along with ice for the cooler. No wonder the muscles in her back have become overdeveloped since I last saw her. When she carries my suitcase and squeezes Juárez and lifts her bottle of beer for a swig, the bird tattooed on her shoulder blade shimmies and struts.

Rita has inherited our mother's curves and even at thirty-two shows no signs of drooping. I got tall, instead, like our father, with all his boney angles. Whenever I catch a flash of myself in some surprise mirror, I can't hide from the fact that my elbows and hips and knees poke out of my skin like a poorly staked tent. But not Rita. Rita is still as buoyant as a teenager.

Rita pops another limp tortilla chip into her mouth and takes a gulp of warm Corona. Apparently, no one has found the time to bring home a new block of ice in honor of my arrival.

"Underground rivers," I say, echoing Rita's proclamation but without any of her enthusiasm. "Hard to fathom." I brush sand from my feet for the nth time this hour.

"That's what's so awesome," says Rita. "They're magical. Wait until you see. It'll blow your mind. Trust me."

And though I don't want to, I do, in fact, trust her. Not to keep me safe—no guarantees there—but to impress me. Rita's schemes never fail to astound, though they have also brought me unacceptably close to death and jail, sometimes both at the same time.

Juárez, who evidently only has the one name, is stretched out on the bed, vacating his throne only long enough to shake my hand and scratch his bare belly like a puppy with mange. Not exactly what I had imagined as Rita's Mexican lover. Now he says in his accented, tour-guide lilt, "Cenotes are holy, Billie." Bee-Lee. "The word *cenote* means sacred well. They are entrances to the underworld. Mayans throw sacrifices into them to please the gods."

He pauses to let this bit of exotic information do its work. If he expects me to be a gap-mouthed tourist, he will have a long wait. The underworld. Seriously?

"Do you consider yourself Mayan, Juárez?" I ask.

"No. Well, perhaps a little in my—how do you say?—in my soul."

"In your soul? Well then." I scratch my ankles. The itch is astounding.

Juárez doesn't let up. I'll give him that. He says, "A few years ago, I brought some scientists to a few cenotes deep inland that my father used to take me to when I was a little kid. He always said there were *fantasmas* there. They found jade and gold. A skull even."

If only it were as easy as this. Pray to the right god. Offer the right treasure. Wish granted. There was a foolish time when I believed that justice and hard work always prevailed. That was before the vacant ultrasounds, the tang of rubbing alcohol on my abdomen, and the relentless needles. Before I endured the hushed decorum of specialists' waiting rooms and Richard's hand rubbing my back raw with his impotent consoling. Now I know that bad things happen even to conscientious people. And even the least deserving can get lucky.

"Whatever," says Rita, clearly done with me and my skepticism. "Sacred or not, you need to see them. I wouldn't forgive myself if I sent you back to Richard without having done this. I won't take *no* for an answer."

"You'll have to. I'm not certified to cave dive. Forget it. I'm sticking to the reef." I say all this as if it will matter to her. Once I started appealing to practical concerns, I had, of course, lost the battle.

Rita laughs. "Certified? You think I am? It's not that dangerous, Billie. Divers have mapped out the whole place with miles of guidelines. They put these little triangular markers on them that point to the exit. You can find your way out even in the dark. You just feel the points with your fingertips. Juárez and I have done it. Gone in and killed our lights and felt our way out. It's easy."

"Easy, huh?" I say.

"*Sí*," says Juárez. "*Muy fácil.* At least until our little Rita got scared and turned on her light halfway back." He winks at me.

"I was just checking on you," Rita says with the same defensive whine I used to hear daily as a teenager. *I was just . . .*

"*Claro.* Just checking on me. I know it." Juárez smiles at me like we are in cahoots, and I smile back, in spite of myself.

"Don't be an asshole, darling," says Rita, joking the way she does when she is most serious.

I don't know how long they have been a couple, but Juárez has clearly spent enough time with my sister to know her quirks. He stands up and gives his faded blue-and-green floral swim trunks a much-needed hitch. I hadn't noticed before that he sports a matching bird tattoo wrapped around his left bicep. I can just picture the happy couple in some questionable parlor getting the His-and-Hers special. Juárez squeezes Rita's shoulders contritely and speaks to me over her head. "At Dos Ojos, Rita makes all the Americans feel so brave. Maybe she forgets that she isn't working now that you are here. Tomorrow let's go to the reef. I'm leading a dive in the morning."

"I have to work," says Rita. Words I never once thought I'd hear out of her mouth.

"Come," Juárez says to me. "While Rita works."

Rita likes talking about her job. In the past week alone, she has arranged camping on a deserted cay for a retired couple from Greenwich, spearfishing for a bachelor party, a trek to Chichén Itzá for a family with three teenagers who spent the entire time waiting in the Land Rover listening to suicidal music, and a visit for three businessmen to a local brothel—although that one was clandestine. Rita says she is only the facilitator—she doesn't bother to condone or disapprove of any of these activities. She tells me that her xenophobic clientele flock to her, trusting her simply because she is American.

"For some of these people, all I have to do is feed them a papaya for the first time, and I'm a hero."

I laugh, but I can't summon the taste of papaya from my own memory. I'm sure Richard couldn't have, either. We're not exotic-fruit people.

"They love her," says Juárez.

"Creating danger in a safe world is an art, *mi amor*. Don't forget it."

Rita and I learned to scuba dive together in a class at our high school taught by a furry middle-aged guy who tried to convince us that the best diving in the world was in murky Long Island Sound, and that he would be happy to take us on a private dive weekend. He'd be especially happy to take Rita. The class was Rita's idea, of course. Who else? Every winter afterward, when schoolbreak rolled around, it was Rita who picked which tropical resort we would go to. Our parents would stake out their territory: chaises longues poolside, beach chairs near the ocean, or high stools at the bar—any place where there was gin to fuel their marital bliss—and we'd stake out ours: the reef, the dive shack, the boat. Year after year. Turks and Caicos. Bonaire. Belize. Most years, most dives, I had at least one moment of panic: convincing myself that my tank was hemorrhaging or that I was getting the bends or having an embolism or that the moray eels were hungry. Rita used to say that I had spent too much time reading the chapter of the dive handbook on risks and dangers. But I didn't let my fear stop me from going along with her. To be her dive buddy. To see whatever she wanted to see. To have fun. Better than being with our parents, that was for certain. By the time we graduated from college, though, Rita had grown bored with coral and barracudas and schools of fish flashing mercury. Bored with us. With me. She wanted something more exhilarating. The wrecks of Bermuda. The whale sharks of the Philippines. Destinations where there wasn't a pool for our parents to bicker beside. Sites that required overnight boat trips. Depths that required rebreather equipment.

When we had each turned twenty-one and our trust fund was distributed, Rita took her share and went diving; I went to grad school. She'd email me from time to time. Sometimes there'd be a new job as a dive leader. Usually there'd be a new man. But by the time my exams ended or a new semester started, there'd be another email from a new locale. The latest and greatest, so much better than the one before.

It has been like this for a decade. Rita coming home only once or twice a year. Sometimes she'd show up for Christmas or on her birthday in June. Within twenty-four hours, she'd track down some old boyfriend from high school to sleep with, or, easier yet, take up with whatever guy I was seeing, as if I wouldn't mind sharing. It isn't malicious, hard as that may be to believe. She just can't cope with our ordinary lives. Can't stomach the world we grew up in. It's all toxic to Rita. But when the memory of the previous visit fades, back she comes like a homing pigeon. Tattooed or pierced in some new, surprising place, ready for fun. Ready to amaze us with her stories. So it was for my graduation and my wedding and even Daddy's funeral last fall. We were all so glad to see her come and so glad, too, to see her leave.

I was shocked when Rita suggested I come visit her in Mexico. Richard and I debated it over dinner. *She must want something from you,* he said. *Or, maybe it's a test of your loyalty.* He pointed his fork at me, a grilled shrimp impaled on its tines. *Maybe she thinks we'll have fun,* I said. He shrugged. The next day I booked my flight. I told Richard I needed a vacation. I told my friends that maybe I'd have a torrid affair with some sexy Mexican guy. I hinted to my mother that I might drag my wayward sister back home to a respectable life. The truth was I wanted two weeks without having to justify to Richard how exactly I spent the twelve hours from when he left for work, his tie origami-crisp, to when he tossed his briefcase on our soapstone counters. I wanted to tell Rita about the lost babies, the last of which even Richard didn't know about. I wanted to tell her about the endless hormone injections and the new sheets that I kept stocked in the closet, still in their hermetic plastic, ready for my next failure. Rita once had the power to make everything better, from my skinned knees to my broken pubescent heart. *Shh, shh, shh,* she used to coo to me. *It's all right, Owl.*

IT TAKES MORE THAN an hour of crisscrossing the parched terrain in Rita's battered jeep, the trees stunted and sparse, to get to the site. Each time the jeep dives into a rut, the dive tanks in the back clang together. It's my designated task to stop this from happening, as if the tanks are torpedoes that might accidentally launch. But having had my hand crushed a couple of times and increasingly nauseated from riding backwards, I surrender to the possibility that the jeep might detonate at any time. I clench the dashboard and keep a steady eye on the horizon.

"Jesus, Rita, could you slow down?"

"You begging for mercy?" This is a remnant from our childhood that Rita brings up too often, as if any sister in history has ever enjoyed that wrist-wrenching game. She slows down until the jeep bucks and sways through the ruts like a boat on swells. The tanks still slam together.

"Fine," I say. "Point made. Mercy." Rita floors it again.

Ten minutes later, we slam to a halt in front of a shack, its door a curtain of beads painted with a Fanta ad. Our dust showers a cluster of scruffy kids in adult-sized American T-shirts playing with sticks. If they mind, they don't show it. Rib-thin goats and a motley clutch of chickens patrol the yard. Heat shimmers above the dirt road. Rita rattles something in Spanish at the kids. They wait for a long minute, then make a show of dusting off their hands before finally moving slowly to the shack, two skinny brown dogs licking at their legs. After another heavy pause, a pygmy-sized woman saunters over to our car. She doesn't speak but leers, showing off a massive gold eyetooth so oversized it looks like she must have picked it up secondhand.

In all our years of family travel, we never ventured far from the resorts. We stayed where things were clean.

Occasionally we made it into small surfer towns, where stoners from up and down the California coast had come to roost. These were a second home to Rita, even back then, and the atmosphere was welcoming enough that I could find a comfortable perch on the perimeter. By night, we slept in whitewashed cottages draped in bougainvillea, fortified on good food and drink, funded by our parents. By day, we chose our adventure. Rita says now that we were spoiled rich girls, implying that I still am and that she has evolved out of this inferior caste. She has told me more than once that I am oblivious to the painful realities of the world. To the plight of the poor. To real people. But my world seems real enough to me. Just because I have ample food to eat and just because I can afford to care about what fixtures I put in my bathroom, doesn't mean I don't suffer. And for all her big talk, I don't see Rita having much more in common with this woman in the shack than I do. I doubt this matron sees an ounce of difference between us. We are both rich Americans to her. I don't see Rita spending her days bringing medical care to the indigenous people of the Yucatán. Richard and I probably give more away in a year than Rita earns.

"You need to pay now," says Rita. I dig through my straw bag and offer her both American dollars and pesos in a card-trick fan. The old woman spies a twenty, reaches across Rita, and plucks out the bill. She tucks it into her dress and then slaps the side of the jeep like the flank of a steed.

"Usually I only give her about five bucks," Rita says. "So you're her new best friend." She pulls down her sunglasses so I can see the tease in her eyes.

"Thanks for the tip-off," I say, flushing. Richard and I had made hard choices to earn our money—choices that involved long hours in cubicles and endless grad school, instead of hammocks and tequila shooters at sundown paid for by a withering trust fund. Where will Rita be when the well runs dry?

A HUNDRED YARDS AFTER THE shack, the arid landscape turns abruptly green, and we lumber on in silence for another twenty minutes. When we stop again, Rita leaps from the jeep and gets busy tugging the tanks, weight belts, and buoyancy vests from the back, the muscles under her shoulder blades shuffling and her biceps flexing. She strips to her teeny bikini and wriggles into a wet suit, yanking a long cord to zip up the back. If I had clocked her, this whole ritual would have come in at under sixty seconds.

"So, what's the deal with the bird?" I say.

"What bird?"

I throw her a look.

She laughs. "You like it? It's a quetzal. Juárez has one just like it. He got his when he turned eighteen." Apparently when they were in Cozumel together she had had a copy made. I have to wonder how Juárez feels about this plagiarism.

Rita says, "It's a Mayan holy bird."

"That'll look great when you're eighty," I say.

Rita laughs again and tells me that old lady hotness isn't her top priority. "*Vámonos,*" she says.

With a tank in one hand and a buoyancy vest in the other, she scampers down a path of flat stones that was completely camouflaged a second before. Now I see a small sign in the underbrush, the size of my palm, scratched with a barely legible number 3. As usual, it's my job to resist this cave dive, resist the thrill of danger, until Rita can entice me to join. Then I have to be both amazed and grateful. And here we are, wherever this is, ready for the second act of the performance to begin. A wave of lethargy sweeps over me and anchors me to the passenger seat, even though my bones are aching for a stretch after the jarring ride. I am a marionette to Rita's puppet master once again. Later tonight we'll be yucking it up at a cantina, telling Juárez about the thrills and chills. I'll be lavishing Rita with intoxicated praise for helping me truly live, once again. This is the familiar happy ending, but at this moment I can hardly stomach it.

Rita returns in a minute for the rest of our gear, and I finally get out of the jeep. I slowly wrestle on a faded cold-water wetsuit she has lent me. It's too short and pulls through the crotch. The suit has been stretched thin from innumerable wearings by Rita's ample breasts so that now the tired neoprene projects from my subpar chest like a bra badly in need of padding. As much as I squirm, trying illogically to shift the abundance of fabric at the top to the shortfall at the bottom, it won't budge, and I can't shake the creepy feeling that I am walking around in my sister's shed skin.

Meanwhile, Rita is pulling small flashlights from a milk crate in the back of the jeep, flicking them on and off, holding them up to her palm to test their brilliance, pitching the runts back into the crate.

"Better take both," she says, handing two little lights to me.

"No kidding," I say. I recheck each light, their filaments barely golden, and clip them onto my vest. Richard wouldn't have considered them adequate as safety lights in our kitchen emergency drawer, forget about the sole source of visibility for me in a subterranean labyrinth. "You really know how to make a girl feel safe."

"C'mon, Billie, I'm all about the thrill, remember?" She excavates a diving floodlight the size of a small trashcan. She shakes it at me in a mischievous, don't-fret-I've-got-it-covered way. "It's gonna be awesome." Her laugh echoes behind her as she trots down the path again.

I feel the pull of Rita's will like a tidal force, building me up, making me just a little bit excited in spite of myself.

The cave is fifty steps down from the dirt road. Inside there is a hole, thirty feet across and full of serene, clear water. It is a gigantic, rain-filled pothole. Along the rim, where the earth once collapsed, a cross section of roots, soil, and ancient limestone is still visible. Leave it to Rita to find a godforsaken place like this and blithely plunge into it. As if she has every right.

Outside the cave, all the jungle's critters—the ones with too many legs or rapid-fire wings or twitching whiskers—are in perpetual motion around trees with prehistoric-sized leaves, themselves wrapped in ravenous vines abloom with toxic flowers. It seems likely that the jungle will ensnare Rita's jeep before the day is out, and we'll be stuck here forever. Around us, the creatures hum as they go about their business, doing the same tedious things they had been doing that morning and the day before. And will do tomorrow. After we are back at the casita. After I fly home to Richard. To the babies that I will somehow manage to have. They will still be at it after my blip of a life, nearly nonexistent in geological time, has zipped past.

Inside the cave, there is gray. The pool is shallow and meager, four feet at the deepest and a little disappointing. Slabs of ashen limestone form the floor and walls. It is a dead-looking place. A believable underworld, I suppose, if you are so inclined, which I am not. Only a few stalwart beams of sunlight manage to pierce the canopy of trees and plants that choke each other to get closer to this improbable source of water. Naked plant roots dangle from the edge of the hole like fishing lines. How is it possible that the well hasn't dried up in the never-ending heat of the Yucatán? Nothing in the cave is living up to Rita's relentless advertising. How I just had to dive here. How it would blow my mind. Change my life. Kick my ass. Rita and her well-oiled pitch.

I slip into the water with just my fins and wet suit, leaving the rest of the gear where I can reach it on the ledge. I strap a weight belt around my hips, clear my mask with spit, and slide it over my face. There's a right order for these things. Stick to the plan every time.

Rita helps me into my tank and turns on the valve. Then I submerge until I am kneeling on the floor of this cement-gray, oversized puddle, just like we used to on the sandy bottom of the Atlantic when we were girls, our bathing suits bulging with rocks to anchor our buoyant selves, the swells moving above us. Rita used to challenge me to see who could stay under longer. I always lost.

Now Rita's hand, cinnamon and sparkling with silver rings on thumb and fingers alike, pierces the water not a foot from my face, snapping me back to her. I follow the invisible arrow from her index finger, and there it is—a tiny gap along the left edge of the pool where the shards of limestone don't quite meet. It is like a seam that hasn't been sewn together properly. It's dark on the other side of the hole, and the entrance is very small. There's just enough room for a woman with a metal cylinder strapped to her back to sneak through.

ONCE INSIDE THE CENOTE, the narrow tunnel widens into a room. Blocks of limestone rest at impossible angles, a dust-covered wreckage. There is no natural floor or ceiling or horizon, just stone slabs jutting out indiscriminately. Everywhere, everything is chalky gray, the color of pumice and old bone. There are stalagmites and stalactites in clumps, formed during some drier period before rainwater flooded the whole delicate system, preserving the formations like bugs in amber. Only these relics tell me which way the force of gravity runs.

A minute into the dive, Rita holds up her hand and gestures for me to turn around. Behind us, through the tiny crack where we entered, is a shock of ultramarine light, glowing like the entrance to Heaven itself. It is magnificent. How could I have doubted? For the first time in two years I stop resenting the cold-hearted God that left Richard and me empty-handed while every day babies are shaken or abandoned or aborted. We can turn back now, and I will be sated. I smile at Rita. She smiles back—I can see the pinch of her dimples around her regulator. That's it. That satisfied, exuberant smile.

We don't turn back, of course. Rita leads us away from the glowing entrance, deeper into the maze of the cenote. I dutifully follow, keeping one eye anchored on the yellow nylon guideline. Every turn we take, there's the line and every few feet, like Hansel and Gretel's breadcrumbs, are small metal triangles. Just as Rita promised.

THE STALAGMITES AND STALACTITES —'mites and 'tites Rita calls them—are lumpy like the sand-dripped towers we used to build, summer after summer, while Mother and Daddy napped in their beach chairs. Some of the stalactites are as skinny as drinking straws, thickly bunched together. Safety in numbers, I suppose. But the stalagmites are enormous fat pillars, thicker than my torso, rising from the depths, stretching nearly the height of the cavern. Only they don't quite reach that high, making me question the integrity of the whole damn place. If these pillars are just for show, what is keeping the roof from caving in, right here, right now? I turn back to look for that calming beacon of blue, but we have gone into the cave zone beyond the reach of natural light.

The water is translucent, but it is dark, too, the kind of darkness that feels gauzy against your face and compels you to reach for something solid—a wall, a body, a bedpost—only here that won't be allowed. Rita warned me that stirred silt will cloud the water for days and I sure-as-shit better not touch anything. There's no organic life to pollute the cave water with bubbles and excrement and filthy biology. Unless my sloppy humanness gets in the way, the visibility will be clear for hundreds of feet. Of course, my flashlight has only a fifteen-foot range at best, so I can't fully make out the gothic scene in any case. Mostly I keep my beam locked on Rita's neon pink legs and let her floodlight do the sightseeing. I'm not interested in the scenery now anyhow, being so busy concentrating on the steady inhale/exhale that keeps me hovering, contact-free, between the clenched limestone jaws. Like in all dives, sound and smell and taste are rendered useless: nothing to hear but the suck of air from my tank and, a moment later, the burst of bubbles through my regulator; nothing to taste but the rubber mouthpiece; nothing to smell. My sight is handicapped not only by the deepening darkness of the cave, but by my mask's obstruction of my peripheral vision. I squint to get a clearer, more complete view of where I am and where I am going, but it's useless.

We follow whatever underworld mole holes Rita chooses until I am thoroughly lost. I never really did have much of a sense of direction. I check my depth gauge and air supply every half-minute, as if the knowledge that we are deeper and I have less air will give me much in the way of comfort. Then we come to a widening of the tunnels. We hover for a minute in this chamber while Rita spotlights the formations. I stop looking. I am not one of Rita's little resort groupies.

Rita raps her knuckles against her tank until I turn to the clanging, then she makes a thumbs-down gesture. Descend. When she dives, it is in slow motion—a languid dolphin kick and down she goes. Beneath me I can see only a blur of pink neon. It's like watching a fish beneath ice, not a woman through glass-clear water. I reach toward this non-Rita, not quite sure how far away she is, and feel nothing but an abrupt drop in temperature. I dip my hand in and out of this arctic layer a few times. I reach lower into the glow, but there is nothing solid. I am still puzzling it out when miniature bubbles rush past my face. I pull back, startled, and stare again into the odd space below me. Then Rita reappears, only inches away, grinning. Even with a mask over her face, Rita's eyes proclaim her latest triumph. My flushed cheeks sting against the cold water. Rita signals again with a flourish: *descend.* And then: *okay?*

When Rita disappears for the second time, I know she won't be back. She will wait on the other side of this invisible wall for however long it takes me to summon the nerve to go through. I hate Rita for knowing how far I can go. As it is, I have waited too long. I am giving her plenty of fodder for teasing at the cantina tonight. So I descend slowly by bleeding air from my buoyancy vest. First the cold water wraps around my ankles as I sink, then my hands, and, finally, as my head goes in, the water becomes a miasma. It is like floating in oil and vinegar. Less than a foot deeper the water clears but is absurdly cold, and there is Rita, bobbing in front of me, still smiling. She gives the *okay?* sign and then points upward. Above our heads is a tangle of liquids refusing to blend, like a roiling, cloud-filled sky. I half-expect to see the hand of God himself point through that turbulent layer. Rita gently stirs the water above our heads. Swirls eddy and curl around her fingers. I fill my lungs with air, making my body float a few tentative inches higher. Clear. Blurry. Cold. Warm. I check my depth gauge. Fifty-five feet. Deep.

I surrender to the grandeur of Rita's cenote then and for a while stop my obsessive monitoring of my air gauge. When I look again I am startled to see I am at half a tank. We need to turn back. We should have turned back already. I show my gauge to Rita, feigning a business-like demeanor. She switches off the blinding floodlight and uses one of my small flashlights while she tightens my valves, then gestures for me to slow down. Rita flashes me her own air gauge, which looks to still be three-quarters full, and then smirks. Slow. Down. If there had been a gesture for *Stop breathing like a mad woman,* she would have given it. Then Rita gestures again, this time inhaling deeply, closing her eyes, and releasing the air slowly, one hand in a yogi pose over her mind's eye while the other illuminates her face from below the way she used to when she told me ghost stories until I nearly peed the bed. I shine my own light on my raised middle finger, and Rita's dimples deepen.

Rita flips the switch on the floodlight. Nothing happens. She stares into its prismatic lens for several meditative seconds. I wait with the rubber mouthpiece clenched between my teeth, chewing it until I can taste the iron of my blood, while Rita reexamines each crevice of the light. She flips the switch once, twice, three times. Then she shakes the light violently and flips it again. Her skinny, pierced eyebrows furrow together. She looks at me and shrugs. Then she points at her little emergency light and gives an upbeat *okay* sign.

I shake my head from side to side so hard I feel a wave of vertigo. Panic percolates in my chest until I cough. Rita points at her own eyes and then at a green guideline in the bottom of the chamber leading to another tunnel. *Look? Okay?* It isn't the one we followed in. Does she know this? Then she turns away from me and swims toward the tunnel, leaving me with not enough air and a light not strong enough to light up the inside of my left nostril. This whole undertaking has gone too far. More often than not, it goes too far. If we were anywhere else—on the beach as children, in the woods as teenagers, at some awkward family function as adults—I would have walked out. It has always been my preferred means of protest. Departure. I can never fight Rita and win, but Rita is like a sun-starved plant, and without me there to pay attention she shrivels up. I learned this early on. Retreat is a weapon. Rita would track me down in our bedroom where I would be drawing, or up on the beach house porch where I would be painting my toenails, or in the library sipping a glass of Chardonnay with Richard. Rita would act like a repentant pony, nudging me until I laughed. Making up. I want nothing more right now than to be back at the casita, giving Rita the silent treatment, waiting for some sort of adequate compensation to be proffered for her incompetence.

My eyes flicker from my air gauge to the guideline to Rita's fluttering fins, not knowing which is the real harbinger of safety. My flashlight can illuminate only one of these items at a time. Anything beyond its small perimeter is night.

Rita slips through another narrow crevice, her neon fins the last glimpse of her. Flick-flick. Gone.

I follow, but the space is smaller than I expected—or I am bigger—and my tank hits the side of a formation, making an echoing clang. I gasp, and my lungs fill with air. I become more buoyant and float into a cluster of stalactites. Their dusty fingers grab at me. I swing my arms wildly and drop the flashlight. It dangles from my wrist, casting its frenzied light at the stalagmite teeth below. Limestone scrapes my forehead and digs into my scalp. I spin my head and knock the regulator from my mouth. I grope in the dark for the missing mouthpiece.

While my body panics, my brain stays focused like a compass in a gimbal. If you panic, you will drown, and what a waste that will be. You still have air, you still have your regulator, you still have a flashlight. Put them together and you have salvation. I close my eyes to block out the blackness and better listen to my brain. My searching hand finally bumps into the regulator and pops it into my mouth. I blast it clear of water with what little air I have left in my lungs, and breathe cautiously. When it comes back deliciously dry, I suck hard like an asthmatic. I recover my flashlight, open my eyes, and look around. The scene is blurry with disturbed silt. Rita's neon is nowhere in sight.

In the panic, I have used up even more air. Without Rita near me to share her tank, it is entirely possible that I will die before I find the exit. I search for the green guideline Rita had pointed to. In the tunnel that she took, I see no guideline and no Rita, just endless gray dust camouflaging everything. Then, in a crevice far below, my searching flashlight beam reflects off a metallic triangle tied to a red guideline. It's the wrong color. It isn't the way we came in, nor the way Rita went out, but it doesn't really matter. Those arrows point out, and I want out.

WITH MY FINGERTIPS HOLDING tight to the guideline and its arrows, I make my way back through the silt. Not one part of me wants to give up. Not one cell considers surrender. I am vibrating like the electrons I stalked in grad school. By the time I reach the same innocent pool where we had started, my air gauge hovers near the red zone and my fingers are stripped raw. I am febrile with adrenalin. Rita isn't there, but resting on the ledge, surrounded by a fresh puddle of water, is the broken spotlight. I retch, a mix of gulped water and breakfast and relief.

Damn her. For leaving me in there when she knew I was running dry. For not keeping one eye behind her. I thrust my fins and mask onto the ledge and shimmy out of my buoyancy vest. The shaking won't stop. C'mon, Rita. Enough.

I check my watch. She will resurface through that crack along the left edge of the cenote. It will happen soon I think, although I'm not sure of the dive's duration. I should have set a stopwatch, of course. Standard dive protocol. If I hadn't been so distracted by this surreal cave system, by Rita, I never would have forgotten that. I wait until enough time has passed for the water dripping off my hands to evaporate and for the puddle around the spotlight to dry. Soon. It's hard, though, to estimate how much time Rita has left. She always breathes as infrequently as a beluga. It is also possible that she has resurfaced in some other pool. I wait on the ledge next to my discarded tank and fins, my feet pruned and frigid.

I unzip the wet suit and pull it off of my torso, leaving the sleeves dangling from my waist. It's colder in the cave than I remembered, and I search for a spot where the sun pierces the foliage so I can warm up. I wrap my arms around my chest. How long am I expected to tolerate this? Rita never could detect other people's limits—her stories run too long, her hugs are too tight, her pace too frenetic. I pull off the rest of the miserable wet suit in silent protest.

After another fifteen minutes, I reconsider my air gauge. I surfaced with about an eighth of a tank left. Maybe fifteen minutes worth. Depending on how deep I go. How fast I breathe. It might only make matters worse to go in after Rita. Which line would I even follow? How impenetrable is the sediment now? Though I know it isn't possible, I hear my digital watch ticking. Its cardiac rhythm counts off the minutes, the seconds, the rapid-fire hundredths, that I have been out of the water, safely breathing the dank cave air, and Rita has been in there, somewhere, looking for me. My heart beats alongside the watch's tick-tick-ticking, its muscular contractions so strong they hurt.

There is a fulcrum-moment when waiting is no longer passive. When waiting becomes an active choice. When the opportunity cost of waiting becomes tangible. You could be trying to find a signal for your cell phone. You could be pantomiming disaster to that Mayan matron at the gate who must know how to call the police. You could be finding a way beyond your phrasebook Spanish—*Excuse me, sir, call the fire department, the pickpocket has stolen my toilet paper!* By now, you could have found out that the woman doesn't speak Spanish anyway; she speaks Mayan, which you thought was as dead as Latin. Wrong again. But no need to worry, Mayans are fluent in the language of panic and desperation and disaster and sacrifice. History gave them practice. She saw Rita come in—impossible not to notice someone like her—and now she doesn't see her come out with hysterical you. She knows the cenote. So, she knows.

You could get that wetsuit back over your shoulders, zipped up by its tail, that buoyancy vest and tank strapped back on. You could use up whatever you've got left. You could keep one hand on the safety line.

You could stand out in the jungle and holler louder than the quetzals and the oropendolas and the vacant, sound-sucking, heat-thick sky.

You could pray. You could cry. Or you could just wait.

A SIXTH SENSE ALLOWS ME to picture exactly where Rita is: jammed head first, legs dangling, in a nest of stalactites, limestone leaving an imprint on her waterlogged cheek. Actually, I can't see this horror as much as I can feel it: limestone against my own cheek, its grit ground into my scalp, the chafing from the dive gear, the flashlight strap cutting into my wrist, my hair Medusa-tangled. And when she stops resisting—she will stop at some point, I know—Rita's hands will curl near her lips, her skin pickled and pale, her body a comma, suspended by water, cradled and buoyant, waiting.

I know what will happen. The police will come. They will check every possible exit from the cave system in case Rita has found a safe place. They will check inside the cenote, too, but it will be too cloudy. They will ask me questions, and I will have to be a tender combination of calm and hysterical. Another part I can play. When they don't find her on the first attempt, they will agree to come back the next morning. No one will say that there is no hope of finding her alive. At least not in English. Out of respect. Maybe they will say it in Spanish. Or maybe they will be making their dinner plans. How will I know? I'll have Juárez come. Juárez with his matching quetzal tattoo. I will need Juárez so I'll know if *la policia* are calling Rita a stupid girl. Or me. More likely they will be talking about the lack of air pockets. They will be running the numbers. Only one tank. Crazy. Eight hours. Impossible. They will send me home—*a la casa*—but I will have only Rita's casita to go to. Rita's sandy, mildewed bed to sleep in. Rita's patchouli-soaked air to breathe. This will be my penance.

Rita knows all about the places where one world ends and another begins. Where change lurks. Where one life is traded for another. Where compromises are brokered. Where sacrifices must be made. Certainly the Mayans knew. Beneath their feet, beneath that parched ground where they built their simple shelters, where their children rocked in hammocks shaded from the dehydrating sun, where crops refused to grow because rain refused to fall, there was a labyrinthine city of water. Down there the greedy, selfish underworld gods laughed at them. Tested them. Punished their transgressions with drought. They taught us to give what we have to the cenote in reparation and supplication—our jade and our pottery and our best goats. Anything that sparkles, anything with the blood of life. Rita would want me to.

The Catch-and-Release Man

The knot in Mrs. Van Vliet's left trapezius is as stubborn as it has been every week for the last year. Glenn works it—that's what he's paid to do—but he doesn't have to think about it anymore. That fleshy walnut is right beneath a constellation of five freckles, hiding under her scapula, and protected by a layer of blubber that makes his job just a little more difficult. He'll never get rid of her knot. He figured that out months ago. At least not until Mrs. Van Vliet stops hunching over her desk for four hours a day and quits chain smoking and finally stops hating Mr. Van Vliet. With clients like this, it's best to just work at the spot, make it hurt enough that they know they are getting their money's worth, and send them on their way until next week. That and listen to them gripe. Nobody tells you in massage-therapy school that more than half of this job amounts to talk therapy. Too bad. That might have scared Glenn off from the get-go and he wouldn't have met June and he wouldn't be making his forearm ache trying to release a chubby, middle-aged woman's misery. June didn't mind all the talk therapy. She took it to the next level, channeling spirits for the clients on her table. Talking about energy and past lives and all sorts of nonsense that Glenn couldn't take with a straight face. Of course, that's exactly why June traded him for Earl. Earl of enlightenment. Earl of spiritual development.

Earl and June are long gone. Taos. Of course. Glenn takes a que será, será attitude to these things. He couldn't have stopped it, he figures. It might have been better if she could have waited until Ripley made it to college. Until things in that department had settled down a bit. But he guesses she just couldn't. Wait, that is.

IF HE HAD CHECKED the weather report, Glenn wouldn't have left his parka back home. Then again, if he did much planning at all, he never would have made it up here to New Hampshire. Planning would have meant thinking about how exactly he was going to break the news about June to Ripley. It's enough of a miracle that he got all of his fishing and camping gear into June's little hatchback. He had had to tie the rods to the roof using inept knots that would have made his Boy Scout of a father roll over in his grave, but other than that, Glenn had packed light. Most of the camping stuff hadn't been used in a decade, but it looked good as new. Only a little moldy. Here and there.

The idea of a fishing weekend had really been Mrs. Van Vliet's inspiration. She and Mr. Van Vliet were heading down to the Turks and Caicos for Thanksgiving. Her son and husband went in for deep-sea fishing. *Fathers and sons, you know. Nothing like a little death and destruction to bring them close.*

And the truth is that Glenn and Ripley had never been so close as those days after Glenn's father died and they went fly-fishing once or twice a week all spring and summer and fall. Ripley was about eleven. June even came along once in a while and sketched while they fished. Ripley quickly became a better fisherman than Glenn. Better at tying flies, better at casting, better at reading the river. June said Glenn was just too earnest. That he needed to be wilier. That he needed to think like his enemy. Like a fish. By the time winter was over, and Ripley was a fully hatched adolescent, he wasn't interested in fishing anymore. At least not with his father. Sometimes he went with his buddies, but Glenn wasn't going to invite himself along on those excursions.

THE DIRECTOR OF THE Redmond School tells Glenn that he'll find Ripley in the back potato fields. The man's a New Age buffoon: Glenn certainly has met more than his fair share in massage classes. Who, exactly, did Glenn think would be running a farm school for wayward boys that June picked out? Better a New Age loon than some military junta type.

Twenty yards into a furrowed field, Glenn spots two boys on their hands and knees digging. If they weren't so big, and if it wasn't so cold, they would have looked like preschoolers in a sandbox. Ripley's got on his orange ski jacket. It makes him look like a pumpkin, but June found it for him somewhere on sale and decided the color was a healing one. Glenn thought Ripley would have laughed at that, but he didn't, and now here he is, the puffy thing swallowing him whole. Ripley's working away at those potatoes, digging them out like a real expert. He's joking with the other crouching boy, and their laughs get bigger and bigger before the sound finally reaches Glenn. His boy is happy.

Last spring Ripley kept getting detention at school. Once, twice, ten times. It was always something harmless. Stupid pranks. Boys do stuff like that, Glenn told June, though he never had done anything like that at all. Still, that's what normal boys, popular boys, do. She didn't see it that way. *It's the start of something really bad. We need to do something right away before Ripley gets into drugs and booze.* Like you, you mean? But Glenn hadn't had the balls to say it. Not back then. June found Redmond online. She met the director and brought home a glossy brochure with pictures of wholesome, freckled boys adventuring in the White Mountains and little white clapboard buildings nestled around a quad. Harvard for the feckless. June unearthed some money, too. A little fund left behind by her parents that was supposed to be for college, but the time for intervention, she said, was now.

Ripley begged not to go, kneeling melodramatically on the kitchen floor. June just cooed at him about how a change of scenery would be healthy. He would love the independence, she gushed. Like college a couple of years early. Glenn hadn't said much. You pretty much had to stay out of June's way when she got going. He put on a teakettle. This was Ripley's fight.

June gave Ripley a big hug, and he buried his head against her shoulder the way he used to with every scabbed knee. Glenn knew then that June had won. After she stood, Ripley was still kneeling on the floor, penitent and pathetic. But she had things to do, she said, in the studio. She couldn't wait around for the kettle to boil.

RIPLEY WALKS OVER FROM the potato field. He hasn't trimmed his buzz cut since he got to the school six weeks ago, and his coarse black hair sticks out of his head like a terrified cartoon character. Glenn reaches out to hug him, but Ripley holds him off by raising his filthy palms.

"Covered in mud," he says.

Glenn nods and worms his hands back into his pockets. His head continues to nod along until he wills it to stop.

"So," Glenn breathes deeply and faces Ripley. "You ready to fish?"

Ripley stares at the ground and says nothing.

"What's wrong?" says Glenn.

"It's just," starts Ripley, squashing a clod of dirt under his work boot, "I thought it might be good if Peter came." Ripley thrusts his chin in the direction of the other potato digger. "He's the friend I was telling you about? In my emails?"

Glenn nods again, this time noncommittally. Since when did he nod so much? What emails was Ripley talking about anyway? Maybe something he had sent to his mother? Who knew. Glenn loves his son, but most of what Ripley says in his messages is crap. Other than making sure Ripley got permission for this weekend away, Glenn didn't bother to read about which teacher was a jerk and how unfair dessert distribution was.

At Ripley's summons, this Peter boy—who Glenn is pretending to have heard of—crosses the field. He is, without doubt, the tallest person Glenn has ever seen. He walks loose-limbed, like a marionette controlled by a lunatic. In his left hand he's got a potato, his fingers long enough to completely encase it.

"Pleased to meet you, Mr. Starkey," says Peter. His teeth are denture straight and falsely square like the ones Glenn's grandfather used to have. He wears his hair in a redneck bob, greasy enough to rake through with your fingers and have it hold its position. Wasn't weekly showering a requirement at Redmond?

"He's got all his own fishing gear," says Ripley.

Glenn rubs the stubble at the nape of his neck.

"C'mon, Dad. Is it such a fucking big deal?"

"Ripley's been a lifesaver for me here, Mr. Starkey. A true friend, sir. If you'd rather I not come along, though, I'd totally understand."

The man-child sticks out his muddy hand for shaking. Glenn takes it. It's hard to say *no* to respect.

"I guess so. If it's okay with your parents, I mean," Glenn says.

GLENN PUTS PETER IN the back seat of June's car, his overgrown legs folding like a carpenter's ruler across the seat. Peter stretches his endless arm along Glenn's doorframe. Its presence, inches from Glenn's face, gives him the unpleasant sensation that he's sitting in Peter's lap.

As they pull out of the driveway, the iron gates clank closed, and the security guard gives a jaunty salute. Peter waves back without irony and says, "May our Lord Jesus Christ bless us with a safe trip."

Our Lord Jesus Christ? Weren't kids at schools like this supposed to be aggressive atheists, tree-hugging pantheists, or at least Unitarians? Glenn has never had patience for religious people any more than he has for June and her crystals. You trust what you see. What you touch. He has always told Ripley that religion is something to be humored in other people. Like the way you play along with Santa Claus. It's usually pretty harmless. But now here's Ripley palling around with this Jesus kid. Glenn sneaks a look at Ripley. He's slouched low in his seat with his head tilted back, eyes closed.

"Why are we in Mom's car?" he asks without opening his eyes. "It's too fucking small."

"The truck's acting up," says Glenn. It sounds truthful enough.

It takes an hour to pass through two towns, each marked only by a flagpole and a mini-mart with fading signs proclaiming the lowest prices on Winstons and Bud. Leftover jack-o'-lanterns rot on dilapidated front porches, their moldy green faces collapsing. Ripley sleeps with his head hung forward. Each time they pass a church, or even just a house with a sun-bleached Virgin Mary in a weedy garden, Glenn holds his breath waiting for St. Peter the Tall to bring up God again.

"Rip was looking forward to seeing you and Mrs. Starkey," Peter says finally. "He says I would like her because she's so spiritual. He says she's real talented."

"Ripley's mom is quite a sculptor," says Glenn.

"Yeah, that too," says Peter with a wistful sigh.

Glenn checks the rearview mirror, but Peter is looking out the window, and the baby-smooth side of his face gives nothing away. He asks, "So, you liking Redmond?"

Peter shrugs. "We all have our crosses to bear, Mr. Starkey."

Glenn suppresses a nod.

Peter just keeps on his roll, "Ripley told me you wanted to be a painter. When you were younger, I mean. Still lifes?"

Glenn blushes. "Oh well, somebody's got to pay the mortgage." He is definitely not going to discuss his lost ambitions.

"I've had a couple of gallery shows, myself. Oils mostly. Abstract stuff. I sold one big canvas for three thousand dollars."

"You don't say," says Glenn. He smirks because there is no damn way that's true. Not even a little. Not even in Peter's Personal La-La Land. Glenn is tempted to bait the boy, get the full depth of the delusion, but what would be sporting in that? Instead, he says, "So, you like to fish?"

"Yes, sir. Sure do. My folks own a cattle ranch, and there's an awesome pond on the back acreage that we keep stocked. Trout mostly. You can practically reach in and grab them."

"A little too easy for my taste."

"Yeah, yeah. Sometimes we go river fishing, too. There're some good spots. I've caught my fair share, let me tell you."

"Done much hiking? Ripley loves to hike. He was pretty much born with a compass in his hand. Learned it from his grandfather—my father. He worked for the forest service for fifty years. Ripley's just like him. Both of them have led me out of the woods on more than one occasion."

"I usually look to Jesus to show me the right direction," says Peter. He produces a gold crucifix from his pocket. It's not a demure kind of cross that dangles from a necklace. It's a good three inches long and shiny. Peter holds it next to Glenn's right ear. It glints in his peripheral vision.

Glenn smiles. "I guess I meant finding your way a bit more literally."

"Me too," says Peter.

Glenn glances into the rearview mirror again. Peter's eyeing him now, eager.

"Jesus shows me which way to go," he says.

"Well, that sounds helpful." Glenn checks his watch. Probably an hour to go. "Maybe Jesus would help me out sometime, too."

"It only works if you truly believe," says Peter, sounding a little peeved.

Glenn shakes Ripley by the knee. "Let's stop for coffee at that diner."

"Jesus doesn't like lying," says Peter.

Glenn slaps Ripley across the thigh. "Wake up, sport."

In the late afternoon, Glenn pulls over alongside a parched field for a piss break. The threesome claim stations by the field's electric fence. A cluster of splotchy cows lay in a circle eyeing them. Every forty feet or so, there's a warning sign with a cartoon of a man touching the fence. Red lightning bolts jab his splayed body. The man frowns.

"I don't get it," says Ripley, zipping up his fly. "How come you don't see any dead cows lying around? The cows at Redmond are so fucking stupid they'd walk right over each other's carcasses if they thought there might be hay in the barn."

Peter laughs. "The fences aren't strong enough to kill you. Just shock you. I've touched them thousands of times back home."

Ripley reaches out toward the thin wire.

Peter grabs Ripley's wrist. "I didn't say it doesn't hurt." Ripley nods and pulls his hand back. Since when did Ripley follow anybody's directions like that? Even as a little kid he'd been the type to stare you in the eye when he stuck his finger in the cake frosting. June used to say it was because he was a fire sign. Glenn thought it was because they were too soft on him, but he could never bring himself to discipline his little boy the way his father and grandfather had with him. Spare the rod and all that bullshit.

"Let's go," Glenn says to the boys, but Peter just keeps talking. "If you let your Savior in and ask for his guidance as you touch the fence, all you'll feel is his strength coursing through your body."

Glenn glances at Ripley to share the lunacy of this moment, but Ripley is intent.

"Oh, c'mon," says Glenn.

Peter hovers his palms an inch above the wire and closes his eyes.

"Lord God, protect me from your electricity and make me one with its power. Show my friend Ripley how your strength protects me every day."

He clenches both fists around the wire. Nothing changes. Peter holds on, his eyes placid, and a cow deep in the field lets out a sonorous moo. After half a minute, he says, "Amen" and removes his hands.

"Jesus-Fucking-Christ," says Ripley in astonishment.

"You got it. Except for the *fucking* part," says Peter, slapping Ripley's shoulder.

"It's probably not even on," says Glenn.

"Try it, then," says Peter congenially. He waits for Glenn to decide.

"I'll leave the miracles to you," says Glenn, but as the boys head back toward the car, he sneaks his hand onto the wire. The current prickles. The burn becomes sharp and insistent, racing up the nerves of his arm. His dental fillings buzz. There is no way he could hold it like Peter had, crazy or not.

GLENN WAKES UP TO the smell of earth in his skin. The morning sun is lost in a gray, dim sky. They camped overnight in a parking lot at the trailhead. The tent was too short for giant Peter, who had to sleep on the diagonal, squeezing Glenn and Ripley into the corners like curled-up kittens. Water from overnight showers had seeped through weak spots in the tent, leaving Glenn already damp and chilled.

He attempts to revive the fire they made last night by sticking in a few pine boughs. The moist branches make a thick smoke but no flames. Most of the camping he has done in life was with his father, whose competence had made Glenn's ignorance invisible. After his mother died, Glenn, his father, Ripley, and June had all hiked together for years. It was on these trips with June that Glenn's father had first taken Ripley under his wing. Glenn had been too busy taking photos of tortured tree trunks and lichen-covered rocks for June's sculpting projects to have time to play woodsman. His father was probably embarrassed by their artistic fervor, or maybe just bored, and filled the time teaching survival skills to Ripley.

"That's never going to ignite," observes Ripley, crawling from the tent, his hair even more vertical than the day before.

"Yeah, you're right," says Glenn, continuing to poke at the smoldering mess and then tossing in a last bough in resignation.

"Where's Peter?" says Ripley.

"Morning prayers, I guess," says Glenn. "Having a convo with Jesus."

"That's cool."

"You believe what he says? Really? Miracles and all that?"

Ripley sticks in dry kindling he has conjured from somewhere, and the fire springs to life. "He's shown me some things I can't explain any normal way, that's for sure."

"Like what?"

"Like that fence yesterday. Or this time when he asked for God's help with a coyote that was attacking one of the lambs, and the coyote just ran away. He's got something magical. For real."

"You know, Ripley, when you were a kid you believed so hard in Santa Claus that when we told you he wasn't real, you locked yourself in the bathroom. You said it was our fault when Santa didn't bring presents that year and you only got stuff from us. You said Santa was insulted. You sent apologies to the North Pole for months." Glenn does not tell this story with the mildly sentimental tone that it deserves but like an accusation.

"I'm not seven anymore, Dad."

"It's just that sometimes we want to believe things that we know are crazy."

"Mom would get it."

This might be true.

Ripley pulls a necklace out from under his collar. A small blue crystal dangles from a leather cord. "Did Mom show you this? It's supposed to align my energy flow. Or something like that. Ever since I started wearing it, I've been feeling way better."

"When did you get this?" Glenn grabs for the pendant.

"What's your problem, man?" Ripley tucks the crystal away, embarrassed. "Mom sent it a few weeks ago."

Glenn knows he should say something about June. Now. He leans closer to the fire.

"Listen, there's something we need to talk about. In private."

Ripley steps back and crosses his arms. He scans the underbrush for Peter.

"Oh, is this where you tell me you're a fag, Dad?" Ripley laughs.

"It's about Mom—why she's not here."

"She's not? I hadn't noticed."

"Listen. You need to hear this," says Glenn. "She won't be home."

Ripley stops and puts his hands on his hips. It is a June mannerism, and it throws Glenn off balance. He feels squirmy under Ripley's glare.

"When you come home at Thanksgiving, I mean," says Glenn.

"Where is she?"

A stick cracks, and there is the unmistakable crunch of footsteps.

"We can talk about it later," he says.

"No, you brought it up. Tell me now. What's the story?"

Peter arrives, crucifix cradled in his pallid, skeletal hands. He appears lost in contemplation. Ripley stares at Glenn.

"She's taking care of her cousin, Clarice. In Florida. She's sick," says Glenn.

He just couldn't do it, not with Peter's sanctimonious eye on him. He sits down on a log and rests his chin on his hands. His eyelids feel weighted, and he lets them close. His face becomes uncomfortably hot.

"This is bullshit, man," says Ripley. He busies himself with the tent.

Glenn makes oatmeal. Ripley eats it leaning against a tree. Peter smiles at Glenn across the fire. It is an encouraging smile, like one Father Grafton used to give Glenn to urge him to spill his childish confessions. He hasn't thought of Father Grafton in decades.

"Are you Catholic?" asks Glenn.

"No. Are you?" says Peter.

Glenn laughs. "No. Not since I was a kid. Not much of a Jesus guy myself. I just meant what denomination are you?"

"I've found my own path to Jesus."

"A la carte?"

"Excuse me?"

"You just pick and choose from all the denominations? A la carte."

"Not exactly."

Ripley says to Peter. "My dad thinks God is just something people make up because they are scared of things they don't understand." He turns to Glenn, "Right?"

"Well—no offense, Peter—but I'd put myself in the don't-know, don't-care category."

"Agnostic," says Peter, as if he has just discovered leprosy. "Not caring is the worst. In my opinion. No offense. My folks are like that. Just can't accept my relationship with the Son of God."

"So you know Jesus personally?" Glenn asks, trying not to sound demeaning, but failing.

"Yes," says Peter.

"Peter's mom thinks he's schizo," offers Ripley.

"Oh, well, yessir, she's worried about me."

"I'll bet."

"But belief in the face of doubt is just one of God's tests. My folks will know the Truth eventually. Or they'll face eternal damnation."

"Okay. Well, then. Let's head out."

THERE ARE TIMES IN life when you can't believe just how royally you've screwed up. Two hours into the trek Glenn realizes that his two-decade-old memory of the location of the river he used to fish with his father is less than ideal. The weather's absurdly cold for November. New Hampshire is a solid twenty degrees colder than home. His pack is too heavy, and he is more out of shape than he knew, having deluded himself with the lie that massage is a physical profession and, thus, no further treadmill time is necessary. Plus, it's raining, and he's wearing jeans. Glenn is chafing in unspeakable places. Of course, the boys have pants made of quick-drying, new-millennium fabric that they're required to own for school hiking trips. Not to mention that the entire purpose of the outing has been ruined by the presence of St. Peter the Creepy. Glenn hears the theme from *Deliverance* in his brain every time he comes upon the boys stopping for a trail-mix break. As soon as he gets close, they pick up their packs and keep moving, like it's some big game of keep away. Glenn is on the verge of vomiting.

If it were just him and Ripley, he would bail. Check them into one of those nasty Bates Motels they saw along the way. Buy him greasy food, turn on the cable, and tell him the truth. But Peter makes that impossible. He and Ripley are having so much fun together, Glenn will be the killjoy if he suggests that they abort the mission. Not to mention that the idea of sharing a scummy motel room with these two boys, or, worse yet, lying alone on a sagging mattress watching ESPN while the boys are having a slumber party in the next room, is too depressing for words. Persevere it is. They'll catch some fish. So what if he doesn't get around to telling Rip about June? If they have a good-enough time, he can come up again next weekend. Or, what the hell, just wait until Thanksgiving. What difference does it make in the end? The key thing is that Ripley and he stay friends.

The next time he catches up, the boys look less amused. They don't bolt as soon as Glenn arrives.

"We haven't seen a blaze in a while, Dad. And this trail isn't exactly cleared. Where's the turn-off?"

The turn-off should be obvious: an enormous boulder sheered in two, like a bowling ball that dropped from Heaven and cracked in half.

"I guess we're not there yet," says Glenn.

"Where's the map?"

"We won't need one. Once we get to the boulder, you just hang a left and the river isn't more than a half hour down."

"No map?"

"Nope." Glenn is still panting from the hike and drops his pack next to the boys'.

"You're shitting me, right?" says Ripley. "So what, exactly, was your plan? Just bushwhack our way to some fishing hole you haven't been to in, what, fifty years? Jesus, you could have mentioned that before."

Ripley kicks the backpacks, and camping pots make a metallic clamor. Peter sits on a mossy log, with his hands dug deep in his jacket pockets and his head down. Probably praying, thinks Glenn.

"Once you see the rock you'll know why we don't need a map. Have a little faith, Ripley. I've been here hundreds of times."

But even as he says it he looks beyond the boys to where several weak trails head off into the brush. All look plausible. None look right.

"You're such a loser, Dad," says Ripley, in a quiet, resigned voice, as if he has just now come to this unfortunate conclusion.

"Gimme a break," says Glenn.

"No," says Ripley. Then he speaks to the drippy, dying foliage overhead. "We hike all the way up here—how many hours have we been humping along?—and NOW he discovers that he doesn't know how the fuck to get to the river."

Peter stands up and holds out his hands, palms down, as if to quiet a class of obnoxious kids. Glenn hates him. More than Ripley at this moment. More than June on the day she left.

"Hey, man, it's okay," says Peter in his smooth preacher's voice. "Your dad didn't get us lost on purpose. Right, Glenn?"

"We're not lost," says Glenn. And what happened to *Mr. Starkey*?

"I've got an idea," says Peter. He pulls his crucifix from his pocket. It's edged with filigree and a slender, girlish Jesus hangs from the cross.

"Let's ask Jesus to guide us."

"Oh, for God's sake," says Glenn.

"I don't know, dude. It's pretty dense woods up here," says Ripley.

Peter just keeps going. "When I don't know which way to go, I just hold my cross on my palm . . . like this . . . and Jesus points it in the direction I should take." He twirls the cross like a game spinner, and Jesus's feet point toward the trail to the left. It's the most overgrown of the lot.

"You can't be serious," says Glenn.

"Absolutely. It's just one of the little ways that my Lord is keeping an eye on me."

"If that thing doesn't work, we could be totally hosed," says Ripley.

"That *thing* is the power of God. Where's your faith?" He wraps an arm around Ripley's shoulders, and Ripley doesn't shuck it off. "Trust me," says Peter. "Have I ever lied to you?"

Ripley's eyes flicker to Glenn, though whether this is because Ripley thinks Glenn is a liar or because he's embarrassed by this bizarre God-will-save-us talk, Glenn can't tell. He looks away.

The grown-up thing to do is to admit defeat and turn this train wreck around. The grown-up thing is to drop off Peter and take Ripley to a quiet corner and talk to him. Then to tell the director that his son has had enough brainwashing, thanks very much. Don't bother sending a bill. The grown-up thing is to go home and wash the dishes and the sheets, vacuum the rugs, pitch every goddamned thing in June's studio, and then change the locks. But Glenn isn't interested in the grown-up thing. He isn't even interested in fishing. He's interested in debunking Peter. Showing his son that this freakish boy is a scammer. Not an artist. Not a second-coming. A seriously schizo lunatic.

Ripley leans a fraction more into Peter's embrace. Glenn wants to tell Peter to get his hands off Ripley. Instead, he steps closer and puts his own hands on Peter and Ripley's shoulders, forming an awkward football huddle. All three bow their heads. Peter mumbles a prayer. Ripley shuffles his feet in a one-man waltz. Raindrops splatter on the upper layer of foliage.

Glenn feels a fantasy rush over him like spring water on a dam—crystalline, cold and fast. There would be Day-Glo rescuers and frothy German shepherds pulling at leashes. Glenn can almost hear the beat of helicopter rotors. Okay, maybe not *that* lost. Glenn scales back his imagination. They would get a little lost, not too bad, Ripley was too good in the woods for that. They could blaze their trail. He lets his eyes rest on the cross still cradled in Peter's free hand. They wouldn't really be lost. But just a little lost. For just a little while. Long enough.

Glenn steps back and slaps his hands together. "I'm skeptical, but let's try it. If we haven't reached the river by nightfall, we'll turn back in the morning. We'll blaze." He pulls out his pocketknife, and cuts off a low branch at the start of the left-hand trail. The knife was a college-graduation gift from his father, before he and June set off on a three-month national-parks road trip. Glenn had laughed when he opened it, at its vicious serrated edge. "This will come in handy if we have to murder somebody," he had said. "Or to cut my leg out of a wolf trap," June had said. His father had only shrugged, "You never know."

"You're buying into it now?" says Ripley. Spittle flies onto Glenn's cheek.

"No, I still have my doubts, but if Peter here is confident . . ."

"Jesus never minded doubt," says Peter. "You can want it to fail, Glenn, but that will just make the Lord's triumph even more powerful to you." He reaches for Glenn's left hand—the right still holds the knife—and shakes it. Peter's rough hand swallows Glenn's small, chilled one. Glenn resists the urge to pull away. His time is coming.

PETER LEADS THROUGH THE dense undergrowth for nearly an hour, using Glenn's knife to mark a path.

Glenn says, "Okay, let's get another bearing. We should be near the river now."

Ripley makes a display of turning away from his father's eager face.

"All right. If it will make you feel more comfortable," says Peter. He carefully collapses the blade of the knife and hands it to Glenn. He pulls the cross from his pocket. They all drop their packs and assume the huddle position. The rain has stopped, and the cloud-covered sun fights to give a little light before surrendering to dusk. Peter stretches out his palm and lays down the cross.

"Quiet," says Ripley, putting his hand atop Peter's. Peter freezes. Ripley bends his head to his chest and pinches his eyes in concentration. He's probably praying, too.

There is a drenched silence. Glenn breathes in as if to speak.

"Shh," whispers Peter, his voice a reprimand.

Then Glenn hears it, too. A rustle. It does not have the rhythm of steps. It's more of a spasm of movement through leaves, like a surprised squirrel rushing away, but much heavier. It stops then, long enough for Glenn to wonder if he heard anything at all. Glenn's neck feels sweaty; he unzips his coat.

"Hello?" calls out Ripley. "Anybody there?"

At first there is nothing and then, again, there is the rustle.

Ripley walks with a stalker's gait up the mound in front of them. Despite his caution, small sticks crack under his feet. Peter follows Ripley, and Glenn follows Peter. Glenn shivers as the sweat dries.

The sound becomes louder and more frantic the closer they get. The rustling mixes with a high-pitched whine, like air bleeding from a punctured ball.

Glenn hustles to the crest of the hill where the boys stand, heads bowed. In a copse of birch trees—shockingly white with golden leaves—is a small deer lying on the ground at Ripley's feet. The deer trembles, muscles twitching. Her front hooves, skinny and split, paw at the wet ground, while her hindquarters rest, as if asleep, behind her. It's like she is two different animals at the same time. Both here and somewhere else. Alive and dead.

Glenn smells the wound but can't see it. Hidden beneath her, no doubt. But the metallic tang of blood curls his nostrils. Dark spots polka-dot the deer's rib cage and neck. Glenn steps backwards and stumbles over a stone.

"God Almighty," says Peter. He crosses himself.

Ripley squats to pet the deer. Her eyes loll back, as if looking away could erase his menacing presence. He holds his hand out to her with a nonexistent offering. Her tongue dangles—long, thin, and muscular—out of her foamy mouth.

"Dad, somebody shot her," says Ripley, with a vulnerability that Glenn hadn't realized how much he has missed. Glenn wants to cradle him. To drape this overgrown boy across his lap and crush him to his chest. To rock away all the pain.

"Give me your knife," says Peter in a commandant's voice.

Glenn looks at him blankly.

"The knife, Glenn. We've got to do something."

The stench of blood, gunpowder, and animal musk make Glenn gag. Bile scorches his throat. The knife is still in his hand.

Glenn should carry the knife to the deer. He should do the deed. It is his knife, after all. His trip. His son. The knife's purpose after all these years seems glaringly clear. He opens the blade, and its mechanism latches with finality.

"No," shouts Ripley, who is now stroking the heaving, filthy flank of the deer.

Glenn holds the knife, slippery in his palm. He steps toward the panting deer, her eyes opening and closing slower now, as if surrendering to sleep. Maybe if we wait just a few minutes, thinks Glenn, maybe nature will take its course.

Glenn imagines how the blade will feel in the deer's muscular flesh. What if it hits bone? How hard will he have to thrust to kill? His father knew these things. His grandfather, too. They had been men of an earlier era. Men of guns and knives. Not essential oils and pressure points. Not paint brushes. Glenn had never even learned to gut the fish he caught. He left that to his elders. And when they were dead, he became strictly a catch-and-release man. June once said, as he and Ripley walked up the porch empty-handed, "Maybe I should take up fly-fishing so at least someone in this house would have the balls to bring home dinner." She had laughed then, but Glenn knew it was the most honest she had bothered to be in years.

Whether he dropped the knife or surrendered it, Glenn doesn't remember. But his hand is empty, and now Peter holds the tool. Glenn looks at his hand with curiosity and astonishment. How had Peter finagled it away without his consent, like a street magician? It is a shameful relief. He takes a step back.

"I've done it before, Rip," whispers Peter. He kneels by the deer.

"No, I'll do it," says Ripley. His voice quavers, but his hand grasps Peter's wrist. Glenn waits for Peter to decline.

"I'll talk you through it," says Peter, handing the knife, hilt first, to Ripley.

"Wait," Glenn says loudly. "You do it, Peter. You're the farm boy."

Peter and Ripley act as if Glenn hasn't spoken. As if he wasn't even there. Glenn feels lightness spread through him like he is evaporating with the deer's steamy breath.

"Dear Jesus," says Peter to the sky, "we return this deer to you. Please forgive us. Amen." Then he turns to Ripley who holds the knife poised above the deer's side. Glenn lets his eyes close.

"No, not the heart. You'll miss. Slit her throat. Be strong and fast."

When Glenn looks again, the deer's head is pitched backwards, her blood coursing onto matted birch leaves.

What was red on the deer now puddles on the ground as black as oil.

"It was the right thing to do," Glenn says, but no one responds.

Peter holds Ripley in his gangly arms.

Glenn scans the woods and spots down the hill, in the direction they had been heading, the split boulder, like a massive stone brain. He wants nothing more than to sleep. Eiderdown and flannel, soft, warm, and enveloping. He thinks of his bed at home, still unmade, its sheets unchanged since June's departure. They carry an increasingly ripe smell of sweat. At first, he clung to June's pillow, her citrus hair. And then, even the thought of stripping those fitted sheets and pillowcases—wrestling them off—became too draining.

The boys break apart. Ripley's face is even blotchier than normal, his eyes bloodshot. Across the puff of his jacket and on his left cheek and on his fingertips are smears of blood. He retrieves the knife from where he had dropped it on the ground. He wipes the blade first on the leaves and then on his thigh. With careful ceremony, he snaps the blade closed and tucks the folded knife into his jacket pocket.

Peter stands. "Look. Jesus has led us to the river. Right there." He points at the boulder.

"Holy shit," says Ripley.

"I've had just about enough of Jesus," says Glenn. "I shouldn't have left it up to that cross in the first place. None of this would've happened."

"That was God's plan."

A smug expression settles on Peter's face. He just can't wait to tell Glenn all about everything. About God. About Art. About Ripley.

"I'll tell you what's God's plan, Peter. God's plan is that me and my kid take a trip together without some Jesus-freak trailing along telling us the path to enlightenment. God's plan is that families stick together. Husbands and wives. Fathers and sons. So we're at the fucking river. So what? That doesn't prove shit. Anybody can get lucky. You believe what you want, but me and Rip are heading home."

Adrenaline pumps through Glenn in hot waves, from his core to his fingertips, until he thinks he could scorch Peter just by laying a hand on the boy's bare skin.

Peter's lip curls. He gives up nothing in response to Glenn's rant, and his voice comes out honey-sweet. "Let's all just have a snack and calm down."

"No. Get your packs. We're leaving."

"No, sir. Let's get to the river. Jesus wants that," says Peter.

"We *do* need some water, Dad," says Ripley, trying to negotiate a truce.

Glenn wants none of it. He ignores Ripley's desperate eyes and stays focused on Peter, like the sun magnified on a doomed insect. "You will do what I say, Peter. Or you can follow your Savior down to the river, and maybe I'll call in the park rangers when I get back to Redmond. And don't think I won't be thrilled to let your folks in on your decision to wait for Jesus's big arrival."

Peter crosses his arms over his chest. "How about I let them know about *you* not having a map? Huh? What do you think they'll have to say about that? Super responsible, Glenn."

"Seems to me they sent you to Redmond for some damn good reason, and I doubt that me not having a map is going to change that. In the end, you're still there because what else are your parents going to do with their poor, poor psychotic son?"

Peter takes a step closer to Glenn and points a long, knuckled finger in his face, but when he speaks his voice comes out weak, cracking like a thirteen-year-old, "You don't know my folks. So you keep out of it. Jesus is watching me. And you."

"Really?"

"It's the truth."

"Leave him alone," says Ripley to Glenn.

"Fine. Fine, I'll leave him alone. But when he grows up, he'll see that Jesus isn't strolling along with him like the friend he never had. He wants the truth? That's the cold, hard truth."

"Truth? That's rich coming from you," mumbles Ripley, the high collar of his puffy jacket swallowing his words.

Glenn's throat constricts.

"I know all about Mom," says Ripley. "I know she's not in Florida. She called me."

"What did she say?"

"That she needed a break. To sculpt. She said she'd come back by Christmas. Don't worry. I can handle it, Dad. I'm not a little kid. People break up. I get it."

"You're wrong, Rip. She's not coming back. Not for me and not for you either," Glenn says. A tremor of recognition ripples across Ripley, but Glenn can't stop himself. He gallops forward with the truth thrust in front of him like a lance. "She went to a commune. In New Mexico. With some guy named Earl. She took my truck and all her sculpting stuff. I haven't heard a word from her." He could have stopped then—mission accomplished, damage done—but he is just getting used to his new weapon, and he takes another pass. "Can you handle *that*, Rip? Do you get *that*?"

Ripley takes a few steps away from Glenn and his triumphant eyes. Away from Peter.

The truth lies exposed in front of all of them, corporeal and bloody.

Peter touches Ripley's arm. "Rip, let her go. She's Judas, man."

"Shut up," whispers Ripley. He pushes back Peter's hand.

"Jesus, we pray to you for redemption of Ripley's mother," says Peter, his hands in prayer, his voice picking up a biblical resonance.

"Shut the fuck up," yells Ripley. "She doesn't need praying. She just needs a vacation. She'll be back. For Christmas. She said so."

Peter says, "But, Ripley, the Bible says: *Do not show favor to any hurtful traitors.*"

"That's enough," Ripley hollers. "This isn't about God or Jesus or the fucking Ten Commandments. You're talking about my mom, man. My mom."

The vermillion sky silhouettes the treetops, forecasting a clear morning. The light is seeping out of the woods already. Behind them the birch copse is already in shadow. Before morning, maggots and flies and carrion eaters will be busy returning the deer to soil. And next week, Peter will still be communing with his personal Jesus in a potato field, dreaming of his next disciple, and June and Earl will still be basking in the New Mexican sun, their palms chalky with dried clay, and Glenn, well, Glenn will still be elbow-deep in Mrs. Van Vliet's meaty shoulder, listening to her guiltless confessions. But Ripley will be back where he belongs: at home, in a normal school.

Glenn wants nothing more than to pull Ripley to his chest, to let the boy weep without shame. But it's cold and it's raw, and Ripley's arms are tightly crossed, his shoulders hunched, and his chin buried beneath the collar of his enormous, insulating coat. Glenn wraps an arm around his son's stiff frame. He can barely find anything solid through all the layers of down, but he squeezes hard, searching for flesh and bone.

Baby Teeth

The boy smiled at his mother wide enough to show off the slot where his tooth had been. It was a big gap, but not big enough for the ridged adult tooth trying to squeeze through and knocking everything else cockeyed in its wake. When he rubbed his tongue over the ridges, which he did at least twice a minute—it felt huge and sharp, something ferocious appearing from inside his body, and it scared him just a little.

He traced the path of a tiny red and turquoise fish in its frantic dance around the tank, dragging his oily fingertips across the glass, making a long, smeared squiggle. "Look Mama," he said, pointing to the glass. "It's my name."

Marina nodded. "Honey, don't touch the glass, okay? It makes a mess."

Marina's husband thought it was too soon for her to be out of the house, too soon to see the other mothers who would be everywhere, like robins pecking and listening, hungry. But what did he know about it, in the end? She wasn't going to cancel on her son now. He had been waiting so very patiently to show off his tooth to Dr. Wong. Besides, she basically felt fine. I'll come, too, her husband had said over breakfast. Just in case. Marina couldn't think what the "case" could be, but she found it impossible to refuse. Will had dropped her and Tyler at the door to the medical complex and gone to fetch coffee. They both needed coffee.

Tyler held a little porcelain pillbox in his fist and examined the fish tank with its neon blue rocks, a catfish suckered onto the glass. Marina had tried to convince him to put the tooth under his pillow, but he had refused. *I need to show Dr. Wong,* he had said. *She'll know if it's good enough.* Marina had promised him it was a first-rate tooth, but he wanted a second opinion.

It was his third tooth to fall out. He had lost the first two—the ones on the bottom—a full year earlier when they were knocked into the dirt at T-ball. Will had decided that it was high time that his son learned to field a pop fly. No better way to get over your fear of the ball. That's how he had learned, on this very same field in this very small town. From his own father. Sink or swim. When Will coached—as he liked to tell Marina after nearly every game—he was careful to be fair to the gangly boys who turned backwards to face the outfield fence and the ones who chewed on the leather strips of their gloves and the ones, like his own, who closed their eyes at all the wrong times. Marina wondered every time Will made this little speech, denouncing the other coaches who were only interested in the talented, what would have happened if Tyler had been one of these prodigies. Had he been a chip off the old block, instead of a chip off Marina.

There was very little Will had wanted that had not come to be. All these good, easy successes had melted him year-by-year, softening his jaw line and his cheeks and rounding his nose and lips. Will's mother had lovingly recorded her son's transition from infancy to middle age in her scrapbooks, neatly labeling photos of her little son like butterfly specimens. His face was more boyish now than it had been in his childhood, softer even than Tyler's who had his mother's aggressive chin and deep eye sockets that gave them both a shadowed, guarded expression.

And so last spring Tyler and Will had gotten to the field a few minutes early to work on pop flies. Will lobbing them into the air and Tyler watching them land nearby while he turned his head away and pinched his eyes closed, glove extended, hoping for a miracle. *Keep your eye on it*, harped Will. So Tyler peeked around his glove looking for the incoming ball. He followed his father's directions and booming encouragement—*that's right, that's right*—and jitterbugged into position, sticking his glove defensively into the sky. Still, he lost sight of the ball in the sun and was shocked by its astoundingly painful collision with his mouth. Out came those little teeth, reluctantly, with a geyser of crimson.

His mother had given him a popsicle to stop the bleeding. It was his favorite, the patriotic rocket kind—blueberry, cherry, and lemon—that would leave his lips and tongue a surreal shade of purple. But this time it also left him nauseated and ashamed.

The popsicles were supposed to be a treat for after the game. One teammate complained. He was a chubby blond with a bowl cut whose father always arrived sporting a tie and dress trousers and coached his son through each at-bat. "It isn't fair," whined the boy. Marina wanted to shame this runty, pig-snouted child into silence, but what could you do with his father clinging to the chain-link backstop? His mother a member of the Old Stonington School Board to boot. Marina and Tyler sat together on the chilly metal bench for the first half-inning. While the teammate waited for his turn to bat, he pointed at Tyler's bloodied shirt and said, "You look like you got punched in the face." A couple others laughed.

Tyler looked down at the bib of drying blood on his uniform and began to cry all over again. Blood was scary, he knew this. Bodies only bleed when broken, so even though his mouth was far too numb to be painful, it must be badly damaged. His mother kissed the top of his head through his ball cap. Kneeling before the boy between innings, his father said, "Okay, now, enough of that." At first he used his quiet, storytelling voice, and then he switched to the voice he used when he came home from work, and Tyler complained about all the things his mother had denied him that very day. It was low and growly and came from somewhere in the back of his father's throat, like a wild thing awoken from hibernation.

His mother said it would be fine, to him and then to his father. "It'll be fine. Go back to your team." She conjured a spare T-shirt from the back of the car where she kept a stash of snacks and lotions and towels. She tried to entice him into it, but it wasn't an Orioles T-shirt. They were the Orioles, and without the shirt, who would know what team he was on? He worried even *he* might forget because every season it was a different team, a different animal, a different sport.

Marina stayed with Tyler on the bench while the Orioles played three more innings, holding the stub of the popsicle until blue syrup dripped over her hand and pooled in the dust. She listened to her husband's kind explanations of the rules to his players. Everyone called him a natural coach. But to her, the way he described it, baseball sounded like a complicated and cruel game of keep-away. They hadn't played baseball where she grew up. Who had the luxury of an endless green outfield? Baseball was for suburban kids. She checked to see if her son was paying attention to the game, but he was swirling the melted popsicle in a spiral in the dirt with the toe of his sneaker.

So. Here we are, she thought.

The choices had arrived single file over the years. Had they appeared all at once, like an army of warriors blocking the road, Marina might have done things differently. But the decisions that had to be made were stealthy. They came one by one and asked her to bend herself just a little bit to accommodate them. A little bending wasn't scary. A little bending to get one step closer to where she wanted to be. Closer to what she deserved. And, oh, she deserved so very much. Her mother had made sure she knew that. So Marina made small payments to her compromise account, evolving ever so gradually from the creature she had been born, to the creature she would die. She had learned that it was unwise to look back at the tortuous road she had taken. Looking back created doubt. Should I have gone left or right? What was on that other path? There was nothing there for her now. Not even her mother.

THE FISH IN THE dentist's tank probably had tiny little teeth, too small to be seen, to eat the smelly flakes Tyler knew were their food. He often raised his hand to feed the fish at school. He had looked for their teeth—proof of their hidden shark nature—but he hadn't seen any yet. Maybe they were still babies?

Tyler had known about the baby growing inside his mother for quite a while. It hadn't stopped them from doing any of the things he liked to do, so he hadn't thought much about it. He thought instead about baking cookies and picnicking by the pond and lying underneath their one big tree so his mother would read him Dr. Seuss and *Curious George*. He could recognize the words for himself now, so well that he knew when his mother skipped one, but he said nothing about these mistakes, for fear that she would stop reading to him altogether once he could do it for himself, the way she had with tying his shoelaces and buttoning his shirt. *Such a big boy*, she'd say, shaking her head like it was a disappointment to her, and then kissing his forehead. *Stop growing*, she'd say sternly and then laugh.

But even before he knew about the baby, he worried about his mother's quiet days when she got lost in her serious books, scribbling in her journal in tight script that he couldn't decipher, reading her magazines with their photos of old wrinkled women and lonely, scrubby hillsides. His friends' mothers bought colorful magazines with pretty women on umbrella-strewn beaches next to water the color of Gatorade, and when they finished flipping through the pages, they'd give them to their children with blunt-tipped scissors. Tyler loved the inky smell of those slick pages and the collages he could make with them, pasting cutouts of good things onto pieces of construction paper: puppies, cookies on trays, and anything with a motor: cars, trains, airplanes, boats. If he made a collage with his mother's magazines, it would be sad and quiet and filled with light gray and dark gray and black, like a herd of elephants. He sometimes wondered whether this shadowy person was who his mother became when no one else was watching.

His mother had been napping in the afternoons. Long naps that they would start together, curled up on his parents' big bed by the open windows with the blinds drawn down, so that they rattled against the window frame with whatever spring breeze there might be. He would wake long before her and try to be still. Once, as they lay there, drifting to sleep and back again, she rolled onto her back and placed his hand on her belly. "The baby's moving." Tyler pressed down hard and could feel his mother's pulse and the gurgles of her stomach, but nothing like the hummingbird's wings she said she could feel. Her belly looked the same as always; whatever baby was in there must be awfully small.

"The baby is a girl," she said. "A sister."

And though she could only be speaking to him, she looked toward the window and the persistent light finding its way in around the edges of the drawn shade and seemed to be telling herself this fact as if she had just discovered it that very moment.

"How do you know?" Tyler asked.

"The doctor told me last week. When he looked at the baby with his special camera."

It hadn't really been a decision at all whether or not to have the ultrasound. Marina was eager to see her little baby—a girl!—swimming in oblivion, sucking her thumb. But she hadn't expected the technician's expression to tighten down with each measurement she took, like a bolt in a socket wrench. *We recommend an amnio*, the doctor said later, smiling, using the shortened name of the procedure like it was a jolly old college pal. *Your insurance will cover it, of course.* And she might have stopped there to consider the ramifications. But wasn't it always better to know more? Wasn't the best of prenatal care what she deserved? Will certainly thought so. In went the needle and out came too much information.

"A boy would be better, but a girl's all right, too," said Tyler, trying his best.

THE DECISIONS HAD STARTED knocking on Marina's door early in life, before she was tall enough to turn the doorknob, so her mother had done the honors. *Yes, of course,* she had said, *my daughter should be enrolled in a class for gifted children. This girl spoke her first words even before she gave up my breast. In English* and *Spanish. A marvel, this girl.* Her mother showed no regret at immersing her daughter in this foreign world with its foreign rules. The only walnut eyes, ebony hair, and olive skin in a world of freckles and blue-sky eyes. Those omnipresent blond bowl cuts.

At parent potlucks, Marina's mother told outrageous lies about hopping razor wire at the border and picking fruit in California. When Marina begged her to stop, her mother said with derision, "This is what they expect. They will give you even more if they think you have come from even less."

"We aren't even Mexican," Marina whispered. "You're humiliating me."

Later, her mother said, "It isn't really much of a lie anyway. It was dangerous coming here. We did take jobs no one else wanted. Papi and I. Jobs we were too good for. Knew too much for. We said nothing about it. We lived week to week. For you and for your sister."

"But you read Borges," said Marina. "Cortázar. Puig."

Her mother shrugged. "Tell that to the landlady."

There were places Marina was taken by classmates as she got older: beach cottages and ski condos. There were other places she was not invited: clubs and reunions and luncheons with well-connected elderly relatives. She would have to be smarter than the rest of them to get admitted to those precious places. And she was. With her brains and a world that wanted to make amends, she couldn't snatch up opportunities quickly enough. Her friends' parents offered their stiff congratulations as door after door opened, making sure to mention the generous donors who had funded scholarships for *girls like her.* Her mother advised her to stay a step or two behind. *You will get further that way. If you go in front, the bullets will hit you first.*

Marina had only wanted to be given an equal chance: poor girls and rich boys, on the starting line together. By the time she made it to Yale, her father cooling in his grave, she let herself pretend that the differences were finally equalized like pressure in your ears as you fall from the sky. Then one day she and her mother took a winter-break expedition to the Guggenheim uptown and ran into one of Marina's classmates. Marina balked for an instant before introducing her mother. Her mother in a winter coat that had needed replacement for several seasons already, her face sallow and her back weary with all the waiting she had done. Waiting to return to a place that no longer wanted her, to friends that had long ago disappeared, to a path through life that would lead up and up, not wind around in endless loops. On the subway ride home, her mother hissed: "You think you are one of them now? *Estúpida.* You think it is only me that they see as worthless? Who will they bring home to their mamas for Christmas? Maybe once or twice it will be you, and you'll stand there, pretending you have nothing in common with the woman who cooks for them. *Mentirosa.* Then someone will ask if you wouldn't mind—sweet dear—telling Augustina please a few things about the roast, just to make sure she gets it right. Maybe at dinner the family will find you amusing. Their boy has brought home a juggling bear. Maybe they will think you are a *puta* sent by the devil to seduce their boy, and he will be thrilled at their disapproval. You will have served his purposes either way. But when it matters, there won't be a dead aunt's ring on your finger, *chica*."

Her mother had been wrong about the ring. But not wrong about the sacrifices required for Marina to become a genuine resident of Old Stonington. How to dress, how to exercise, how to decorate, how to raise a child. There were rules to be followed on the road to perfection, and Marina had agreed to them all, one by one. "You'll be able to try again soon," said the obstetrician. "It's just a fluke. No reason to worry for next time." *It's not a fluke,* Marina thought angrily, *It's a girl.* And her mother's voice hissed in her ear: *You are one of them now?*

THE TOOTH IN THE porcelain box made a satisfying clicking sound when Tyler shook it. He was proud of his rabbit tooth, as Grandma Albright had called it. It had come out without blood or tears and now would be safely delivered to the Tooth Fairy. It was an incisor, pearly white and hard-shelled like a Chiclet. The first two, the ones that had never been recovered from the dusty infield, had been yellow and flaky. No matter how hard Tyler had brushed them they always had looked like cheese. Still, he had wanted them after they fell out, wanted them desperately, for the Tooth Fairy. His father had suggested, not unkindly, that he had probably swallowed them—his head had been tilted far back—and Tyler wondered with horror if they would always be rattling around in his stomach, indigestible shards that would tear at his intestines.

He had awoken in the middle of the night and screamed for his mother. "They're gone," he wailed. "I've lost them. They're inside me. Chewing on me."

His mother had been groggy, nearly anesthetized. "Who's inside you?" she said.

A trickle of blood, sticky with spittle, ran down the boy's chin.

"You're bleeding again," she said.

He touched his slippery chin. Even in the night-light's anemic glow he saw the red on his fingertips and sobbed. The bleeding worsened, and his mother ran to the bathroom for a face cloth.

Tyler knew, of course, that his teeth had not been found on the field. They had searched before and after the game, in the grass and on the base path, but like all horrors, it wasn't until the middle of the night that the weight of this failure came to him full force. No teeth meant no Tooth Fairy, and no Tooth Fairy meant no coins for him. And the Fairy might be angry with him for not giving up his teeth as he was supposed to, and, thus, might deny him money for his other teeth, too. His mother assured him that the Tooth Fairy never holds a grudge and, besides, she had a surplus of boys' and girls' teeth.

"What does she do with all the teeth?" Tyler needed to know.

Marina smoothed the blankets. She pushed hair from her son's damp, freshly washed face. The Tooth Fairy hadn't been part of her girlhood either. It was Ratón Pérez, that mouse who turned teeth into coins overnight as they sat in glasses of water on your bedside table. Who knew what this American Tooth Fairy was supposed to do with her loot? Her son's friends had crisp ten-dollar bills under their pillows, a single baby tooth worth as much as an hour of her mother's time.

"Well . . . what do *you* think she does with them?"

The week before, Tyler had seen his little cousin, only six months old, with tiny teeth popping out of his swollen gums. His aunt had told Tyler that the teeth were planted inside the baby's jaw when he was still inside her tummy, and now that they were needed, they would emerge. *Like tulips in spring,* she had said. Tyler had mulled over who had placed those teeth in that tiny baby jaw, and now he thought he knew.

"She puts them in babies' mouths," he told his mother with confidence. "She recycles them. Like soda bottles."

His mother put her hand over her mouth, and her dimples pinched in her cheeks.

"That sounds good to me," she said.

"But you don't get it," he whined. "That's why she'll be mad. The same way Daddy gets mad when we throw out the bottles instead of cleaning them for the recycling man to take."

Tyler felt a tingle in his nose, and tears came to his eyes again.

"No, she'll never get mad. There are so many teeth to collect," said his mother. "It's a big job. She has more than enough to choose from. I bet she only chooses the whitest, shiniest teeth for recycling. She won't even miss them."

Tyler wiped his eyes with the back of his hand and rubbed his tongue over the fleshy hole where his bottom teeth had been. He considered whether those teeth had been too yellow to be Tooth-Fairy material anyway.

THE PILLBOX WAS SHAPED like a molar and could stand on its four little roots. The crown of the tooth was a hinged lid with a golden clasp. Tyler tapped it against the fish tank, trying to get the attention of a black molly hiding in a fake pirate ship.

The porcelain box had been a gift from Marina's mother-in-law when she came to the maternity ward after Tyler was born. Mrs. Albright had warned Marina—as if she could not tell for herself—that the box was European, expensive and fragile, and not at all suitable as a child's toy. If it was intended as a gift for the new mother, Marina had no purpose for it either. Once a tooth had been whisked away by this new Fairy, Marina could scarcely enshrine it on her bedside table where any inquisitive child would eventually look. Not that she had any desire to save the grotesque little remains; it would be like preserving nail clippings. The hair of the dead. So she gave it to Tyler last spring despite her mother-in-law's warning, to soothe his sorrow at having lost two teeth in a dirty infield. He adored its adult delicateness and showed it with pride to his grandmother the very next day.

Tap, tap, tap. The receptionist said, "Be careful, there, you wouldn't want anything to break. Fragile, fragile."

She frowned, and Marina felt a flush rise up her neck.

"Come here," she said to Tyler, and he clambered onto her lap. He had become too heavy for this. Fidgety, too.

"Pony ride? Please?" he said and bounced a little on her knees to give her the idea. He was too old, he knew, for pony rides, and he never would have demanded one in the presence of his friends, but here with just his mother it suddenly seemed necessary. When she gave pony rides to his other little cousin, Amy, she moved through each gait, faster and faster, until, at a frenzied gallop, the girl's pigtails flapping, his mother would spread her knees and tilt Amy's body forward until she tumbled onto the soft carpeting. Her ruffled skirt would flip over her head and expose her matching bottoms. A squeal of shocked laughter would erupt. His mother used to do this for him. No doubt she would do it for his new sister, too. Tyler bobbed a couple more times to remind his mother of his request.

She swiveled his knees to the side. "Not right now, honey," she said. "I'm not up for pony rides yet."

Tyler's shoulder jabbed painfully into her breast. He curled into a ball on her lap, his head tucked beneath her chin, eyes closed, and she wrapped him in a hug. She kissed his wiry hair, the color of burnt caramel, so much like his father. If he had been a girl, would he have had her hair instead?

Will finally arrived with the coffee. Marina smiled wanly at him and sipped it, careful not to spill on the boy in her lap.

Drinking coffee at the dentist's office seemed as flagrant a rule violation as handing a child a lollipop on the way out the door, but the coffee had just the right amount of cream and sugar. Will always had been good at remembering just how everyone took their drinks, nearly priding himself on it, even if he couldn't remember birthdays or anniversaries or his nieces' and nephews' names. Her foggy head needed clearing, and she sipped again.

"You okay?" he asked.

She nodded.

"I saw Billie Anderson-Hayes at the coffee place."

"I owe her a call," Marina said. There had been several messages.

"She asked about you. You missed some parents' association meeting."

"About the auction."

"Yeah, that's it. I said you would call her."

Marina nodded. Billie Anderson-Hayes—with her hair professionally blown out once a week and her unsolicited gardening advice and her four children as evenly spaced as fence posts, one a year—no room for a misstep there—Billie could go to hell.

"I thought after this we could all go out for lunch? If you are up for it," Will said.

"If you want to. I was thinking of bringing him to school for half a day . . ."

"I don't want to go," said Tyler, fake-drowsily, his eyes still closed.

"Your friends must miss you. You were already out half of last week while you were at Grandma's."

Grandma Albright's house had been stale like an attic in summer. She kept dentures in a cup on her bathroom counter. They had hard pink gums and extra white teeth, far bigger than Tyler's baby teeth. They looked, to his surprise, very much like Grandma even though they were only a tiny piece of her. The teeth frightened him, the way plastic skeletons did, like someone had stolen all the living parts and left just the soulless dregs behind. To make them less spooky, he had held the teeth up to his own mouth and pretended to talk, watching the effect in the mirror. Then he'd made the teeth laugh. *Har-har, har-har.*

He heard Grandma before he saw her. "Show some decency," she yelled. Without teeth to contain it, her tongue flopped unrestrainedly and her voice spewed out, wet and garbled, especially on those hissing consonants. Tyler wiped her spittle from his cheek, thinking of pit vipers, and dropped the strange, disembodied contraption back in its cup of seltzer. He had wondered desperately when his mother would rescue him.

"What's one more day going to matter? It's only kindergarten," said Will.

He wrapped his arm around Marina's shoulder and squeezed until the flesh in her arm ached like the rest of her and the coffee in her right hand threatened to spill. She stood up, placing her son on his feet and the coffee on the magazine table. Her husband's arm stayed outstretched across the chair back, leaving a negative image of where she had just been, like the faint impression of her body after she rose from their rumpled bed.

"We should all be together, as a family," he said. He tried to pull his son onto his lap, but Tyler knelt down at a plastic tub of LEGOs instead.

"Should we?" Marina said. She picked up her coffee and watched the cars in the lot, oversized minivans and SUVs trying incompetently to maneuver into compact spaces. She yawned a bit loudly.

Tyler had expected the tiredness to stop now that his mother was home from the doctor. He expected that she would give him underdogs on the swing the way that he liked.

That she'd get up out of bed or off the couch and play—really play—not just insist on boring old story-time and puzzles. That she'd make cartoons off-limits again. But it had been a long time at Grandma's—such a long time—and, if anything, his mother seemed even less his than she had before.

THE ROOM THE HYGIENIST showed them into was too small for so many bodies. *This is ridiculous,* thought Marina. *What child needs both parents for a cleaning?* She sat down in the molded chair in the corner, reserved for mothers, and let her husband stand next to her, leaning awkwardly against the wall at the foot of the patient's chair. Tyler kicked his heels against the padded vinyl footrest, and flecks of playground dirt accumulated on the plastic cover like dandruff. His father brushed them to the floor before anyone came in.

The fluorescent lights in the dentist's office were shockingly bright. Tyler counted the birds twirling in the mobile suspended above the chair. There were twenty-two swooping seagulls, balanced against each other, spinning in the breeze from the air-conditioning vent. Two weeks before, he and his mother had sat on the floor of the new nursery, and she had shown him the mobile that once hung above his crib. How much the baby would like it, just like he had, she had said. The mobile had little wooden characters from the "Hey Diddle Diddle" rhyme, hanging from a crescent moon. *It was Daddy's when he was little, too.* Tyler hadn't remembered it, though he said that he did. She wound the music box inside the moon and it played a tune. *It's mine,* he had said, grabbing it roughly from her hands. His mother hadn't objected. She had stood and brushed her hands across her skirt. *I didn't know you could be so selfish,* she said. Tyler had wanted to retract it then. An egg of shame bounced around in his belly. He put the mobile back on the floor. *Take it,* said his mother. *Since it's yours.* Tyler wanted to tell her that he really was excited for this new person to arrive. To tell her how he would play with the baby. And then his mother would stroke his cheek and squeeze his hand. But the lies wouldn't come. He ran to his room and sobbed. *Please, God, please, God, please: No baby.* He stuffed the mobile into his pajama drawer.

For several nights after that he had waited for his mother to report to his father what a bad, bad boy he had been. On the fourth night, he heard his parents in the dining room using their after-bedtime voices. These were deeper and blurrier and lacked the lilt that they used with him. Worst of all, they were unpredictable: the words and their tones never quite matched. He heard his mother say, *No.* Loudly. She sounded like she did when he tried to run across the street without holding her hand. And then she said, *It isn't that easy.* Softly. His father said something quietly. Then there was the sound of crying. Tyler put his hands over his ears, but his father's business voice cut straight through. *This isn't a small thing. It's a defect, Marina. A defect. A mistake. Don't you get that?*

Then his mother stopped crying. "That's not what my mother would have said."

"Maybe not," agreed his father. "We'd be burdened with it the rest of our lives."

There was low talking then that Tyler couldn't make out even when he took his hands away from his ears and tiptoed to the door and stuck his head into the hall, straining until he could hear the hum of the dimmed hall light. When he heard his parents moving toward the stairs, he slid back into his bed and pinched his eyes closed.

"What will they say?" his mother said.

"Who?"

"Everyone. Everyone will know what we did."

"Tell them you lost it."

"I don't want their pity."

"Would you rather tell them the truth?"

Tyler got out of bed and buried the mobile beneath winter feety pajamas he hadn't worn in months.

THE NEXT MORNING HIS mother looked at him blankly over his Froot Loops. They were supposed to be a treat, but Tyler only pushed the little swollen rings around the bowl with his spoon until they became inedible. His mother was still in her robe, pink and striped, the one he and his father had bought downtown for her for Mother's Day. She wore her glasses. They were thick and slid down her nose every time she looked into her coffee cup. The dark plastic frames transformed his mother into the crazy lady who worked at the library. This was the time to tell her how sorry he was. But the crazy lady who had taken over his mother's chair would probably just shush him anyway. She wouldn't swallow him up in her fresh bread smell. Then both Tyler and his mother, at the same instant, heard the shifting of the bus at the bottom of the hill and its accelerating groan. Jacket, backpack, kiss, squeeze.

On the bus, Tyler decided he would make amends. He would make it better. He would return the mobile to his mother as soon as he got home. He would show her how good he could be. His plan was a soft furry thing he cosseted the whole ride to school and later on a bench in the playground. It was a lonely, jostling day trying to keep his idea alive and not get yelled at by mean Mrs. Pierce. But in the end, it slipped away anyway. *Swish.* First, there was a cold swimming lesson at the club and then hours and hours of cartoons at home. His mother offered no explanation for this indulgence. She just turned on Nickelodeon without even telling Tyler to hang up his jacket and put his swim stuff in the laundry room. He kept the volume low so she wouldn't notice when one show ended and another began, but she wasn't in a noticing mood anyway. She hunched at the kitchen counter with a newspaper and tea. Tyler turned the volume down a little lower on Mr. Krabs and Patrick and forgot what he needed to do.

A WEEK LATER GRANDMA PICKED Tyler up from school and on the way to gymnastics she said, "Mommy and Daddy had to go to the doctor today. You'll come to my house for a sleepover. Won't that be fun?" One night turned into four. The doctor's office wasn't *that* far away, but Grandma told him that good boys mind their own beeswax. When Grandma finally brought him home, his house smelled funny, like chlorine at the pool. Did it always smell this way, and he just hadn't noticed before? His mother was in her bedroom with the door closed. Grandma knocked, peeked inside, and then told him with a puckered face that he needed to play nicely in his room before dinner. His room smelled clean, too, like the rug powder that the cleaning lady used. But it was more than that, too, he realized. His room felt brand-new. Someone had reorganized his closet and dresser and neatly realigned the spines of his books. Dozens of LEGO men stood at attention, arms locked at their sides, along his windowsill. A regiment. Tyler checked on the mobile in a panic. The pajamas in the drawer were in a neater pile, but the mobile, to his amazement, was right where he had left it: the dish tangled up with the spoon.

That night, his mother sat on the edge of his bed. She kissed his forehead and each cheek. "*Besos,*" she said.

"I missed you," he said.

"I missed you, too, little man."

They sat very still and from the kitchen Tyler could hear his father saying good night and thank you to his grandmother.

"If there's anything at all I can do," she said.

"So," his mother said.

"So," said Tyler.

DR. WONG PERCHED ON a padded stool next to Tyler's reclined head. Her hairline had prematurely receded halfway up her scalp, so he could see the hard shell of her bare skull above her forehead. She wore what little hair she did have in a stiff, stubby ponytail, sticking straight out from the back of her head. When she rocked forward and back, to look in his mouth, she looked like a bird pecking a puddle for a drink. He wanted to tell someone this but didn't know if it was one of those things that his mother would smile at and his father would say was rude. It could be hard to tell.

Dr. Wong announced that she would count his teeth and then poked around each tooth with her needle tool, even where his bunny tooth used to be. He waited for it to hurt, but it didn't.

"He has an underbite," said Dr. Wong. "He should see an orthodontist." She glanced at Marina and then at her husband who nodded with too much seriousness.

Dr. Wong had mentioned this underbite before, and Marina had always politely ignored her. The dentist knew her audience, she supposed. Of course, the father, at least this father, would want perfect teeth just like his own. All the smiles in town were as straight as his. Generations of engineered dental perfection. A dentist's dream come true. Dr. Wong had probably noticed Marina's crooked eyetooth during the very first appointment and surmised, correctly, that she would be a tough sell. Marina's mother had always told her that the imperfection made her look mischievous. "You could get that fixed," Will had said to her years ago, before he was her husband and was just one of several possible choices worth considering. They were lying in bed, still intertwined. He ran his hand over her lip, over the spot where her tooth was hidden. "It wouldn't be that expensive," he said. She had smiled, closed-lipped, at him. "If you want, I mean," he said, sensing his misstep. "It doesn't look bad or anything."

"I don't want," Marina had said, but after that she did not part her lips when she smiled for photographs.

"Look," said Dr. Wong, pulling back Tyler's bottom lip to reveal the two oversized teeth, already badly overlapped, that had sprouted from his gums. "See. Like I said. All white. No enamel defect like those baby teeth."

In addition to the ones on the bottom, Tyler's canines and a couple of molars were blotchy and yellow. They tended to rot, too. Dr. Wong had diagnosed it on their first visit. It was a defect, formed in utero. Usually caused by a mother's vitamin deficiency. "You see it in poor countries all the time," Dr. Wong had said with the confidence of experience. Then she saw the expression on Marina's face. "Not that you . . . It's no big deal. The adult teeth come in perfect." Marina wasn't thinking of poverty, though. No, she was thinking of the daily glasses of wine and mercury-soaked tuna melts that she had wolfed down when Will was working late at the firm and even a cigarette or two when her sister came to town. Why had she even bothered with those prenatal horse pills? First, it's the teeth. What else had she done wrong?

Dr. Wong rummaged through a drawer.

"What flavor you like?" she asked. Her accent was still thick at times. Marina had a soft spot for Dr. Wong and her dropped auxiliary verbs and missing indefinite articles, even if she did push orthodontia. Her husband, though, would be unimpressed. Later he'd quiz her on whether she had checked out Dr. Wong's credentials. She had. A dozen years of marriage had taught her that much. Dr. Wong had a diploma from Tufts. When she had asked, other mothers had said that they were sure Dr. Wong was very good, but really, why take chances on something like that? Marina had ignored them. Dr. Wong reminded her that there was a world beyond their suburb, outside their deluxe aquarium tank. Marina had been there, too. She had started there. So had Dr. Wong. Marina often wondered how Dr. Wong had come to be here: in this pristine office with its cheap Americana prints and its standard-issue black mollies and *Highlights* magazines. Did she miss wherever she had been a girl? Marina imagined it to be a place of fertile chaos: alive with car horns and sizzling meat, squealing metal from a tram and demanding, mellifluous voices, all baking under a merciless sun. She wondered if she would ever get to Asia. Would Dr. Wong ever get back? When her own mother had drunk her Mendoza wine all the way down to the dregs, she would say, *It doesn't matter if you go back, you don't ever get back.*

Dr. Wong was saying: "Strawberry, pineapple, blueberry, bubble gum, mint—"

"Mint," said Tyler.

"Ah, mint. So grown-up. Such a big boy." She nodded at the wisdom of his choice to his father, who looked up from his iPhone in time to smile. "I have two girls," said Dr. Wong. "They always chose bubble gum." She grimaced. Will chuckled and dropped the phone into his pocket, contrite.

"Now I'll clean your teeth. Let's get rid of all those sugar bugs. They make cavities." She held up an electric brush and put some of the mint paste onto the tip. Then she held up a thin plastic tube. "You remember Mr. Thirsty? He'll suck up all the water in your mouth." She pressed the light suction against the boy's palm. "See. Doesn't hurt."

Dr. Wong moved tooth to tooth, Tyler holding his jaw open so wide that it ached. The toothbrush whirred and Mr. Thirsty sucked. When the boy's tongue got in the way, Mr. Thirsty snarled and belched until the dentist repositioned it. He tried hard to be in the right place because Mr. Thirsty seemed voracious.

Marina wished her husband would leave the room. It was becoming hot. She needed space. Last week, for the procedure, her obstetrician hadn't let him come in. Against regulations. Or so she had said. That was one thing to thank God for. If he had been there, he might have tried to massage her shoulder like he was now, squeezing hard enough to reach the bone. "Ouch," she said and patted his hand. He then began to stroke her biceps instead, unable, apparently, to just let his hand rest still. The rubbing hand was insistent. A constant reminder of its presence. I am here. It was like a rough tag in a T-shirt, chafing against your neck, irritating. You try to ignore it until you can stand it no longer and rip it from the seam, leaving a little hole behind. Tyler was hyper-sensitive to itchy-scratchy things, too. Another thing that he had gotten from her. Her underarms were sweaty. She shrugged Will's hand away as she removed her cardigan. "Hot," she mumbled. She leaned against the opposite arm of the chair, outside of range.

The sound of the dentist's tools mesmerized her. She felt groggy. She hadn't slept properly in weeks. First, there had been the anxiety of the decision-making and then the procedure and then all of this. Her eyelids began to droop. The muffled voices of her obstetrician and the nurse bled into her mind. A role reversal, she had thought at the time. The woman doctor, the male nurse, their soprano-baritone duet. *That's right. More suction. Here? Yes, that's right.* The bright lights of the procedure room and that sound: motor and vacuum and congestion. Was it real or her imagination? *Almost there, Mrs. Albright. Almost done. Try to relax. You feel relaxed?* Mmm-hmm. Very relaxed.

She awoke with a start back in the dentist's office, her head whiplashing. Her husband was prodding her shoulder again. His face was pale in the fluorescent light. "I've got to get out of here," he whispered, waiting an instant for her approval.

"Yes, go," she said. "It's cramped in here."

"I'm sorry. I just can't . . ." He gestured to Tyler and the dentist. The whirring and sucking. "I've got to get out of here," he repeated and walked from the room.

Tyler's eyes followed his father, rolling far back in their sockets, until he could see the soft fuzz of his own eyebrows.

"Good job," said Dr. Wong. "I'm so proud of you. What toothbrush you like? They all light up." She pushed a fleshy rubber button on the end, and a toothbrush handle glowed yellow like a lightning bug's abdomen. Tyler picked blue.

"All done?" asked his mother. The dentist nodded. "Great. Let's go."

Tyler looked at his mother wide-eyed.

"What?" He looked down at his balled up fist in his lap. "Oh, right. Tyler wants to show you something."

Dr. Wong pulled down her facemask until it dangled from its elastic strap around her neck. Tyler held up the porcelain box.

"Such a pretty box!" said the dentist with feigned enthusiasm, misunderstanding the boy's intent. "Where did you get such a fancy thing?"

"My grandma." Tyler fussed with the tiny latch to get it open, rushing before he lost the dentist's attention.

"Let me help," said Dr. Wong. She opened the box and saw the boy's gleaming incisor. It was one of his white baby teeth, not the stained ones that looked like they belonged on Grandma's terrier.

"Ah! What a tooth," said the dentist. "I'm so glad you showed it to me. Now you'll give it to the Tooth Fairy?"

"Is it good enough?"

She glanced at Marina for translation.

"For the Tooth Fairy," said Tyler. "Is it white enough?"

"She'll like it very much," said Dr. Wong. The latch clicked as it locked. "Give you a dollar for it."

"Is it okay for the baby?"

"Baby?"

"Tyler wants to know if the Tooth Fairy will use this tooth for a new baby."

The dentist furrowed her brow.

"When she puts the teeth in the babies' mouths," said Tyler. "You know, the babies in ladies' tummies."

Marina nodded her head encouragingly.

"It's a perfect tooth. Perfect for a baby," said Dr. Wong.

Tyler beamed. "See, Mama," he said. "It's for our baby."

That night he would put the box under his pillow. The Tooth Fairy would fit it right inside his baby sister's mouth where the defect was, and his mother would be herself again. And he would get a golden dollar coin. Just like he had before. His father would take him to the five-and-ten, and he would spend it on Tootsie Pops and a mega-bouncing rubber ball.

"Congratulations," said Dr. Wong to Marina, smiling.

Marina said demurely, "No, no. Kids, you know. Always with the imagination." Then she patted her son's thigh, and he knew to say nothing. He bit down hard on his tongue with his sharp new tooth and tasted the tang of blood.

"Time to go, little man," said his mother.

"I'm not your little man," he said. It was all he had.

His mother laughed in the tinkling, insincere way that she used with other mothers and Grandma and baggers at the check-out who put the bread on the bottom and the cans on top.

Dr. Wong handed the box back to him. "I'll see you in March then."

On the way to the car, to where his father was waiting with the news station on the radio, his mother held his hand too tight, until the latch on the box pinched a blood blister on his palm. He wouldn't ask her. Not now. Not ever.

Sirens

Lake Wecausett is long and skinny and deep, as if some tremendous beast clawed it out of granite. It is an inhospitable place, but that didn't stop Celine Genette's grandfather from building a summer retreat on one of its stony ledges. The camp was constructed of rough-hewn timber, as if it aspired to be a woodman's hunting lodge, but its fanciful décor—sheets of birch bark, endless wood paneling, and quirky, twiggy furniture—exposed its true identity. A little girl's fairy house on a grand scale.

Celine was born at Camp Five Pines, and the two of them, woman and camp, have grown old together, like spinster sisters. Trees now obscure the once-enviable view from the camp's grand porch, but the encroachment has been slow enough, and Celine has been addled enough, that she hasn't much noticed the change. To her, it is perpetually 1958: she is still thirty-nine, summering at Five Pines with her shell-shocked brother, Ted, who never quite returned from the War. In Celine's stalled reality, this day in late August is Ted's forty-third birthday. It's the end of another summer season. Wealthy camp owners like the Genettes will soon head back to the city. The rest, like Stanley and Betty Merrill from across the lake, will hunker down for a long Adirondack winter. But tonight, the Merrills are coming for cocktails and cake. Celine will wear her pink linen sundress, the one Stanley Merrill says makes her look radiant.

If Celine concentrates, sometimes she can see into another world. There, she is old, and Ted has left her behind. This other reality flashes before her like trout darting beneath November ice. Brilliant but elusive. She can remember bad things that have happened in the world: assassinations and terrorist attacks and children with guns at school. Her parents, her sister, her friends: all gone. In this other world, Celine's niece, Alice, has come to drag her away from Lake Wecausett. To put her in that nursing home. Alice has brought along her teenaged daughter. Her name is Nan, but Celine keeps forgetting that. Nan looks so much like Celine once did, it is impossible for Celine not to believe she is watching her own reincarnation.

Nan's old bathing suit is having a hard time accommodating her ever-enlarging breasts. They seem to have grown again overnight. The teeny bikini will upset her mother, Alice, (who is a prude) but even more her Aunt Celine (who certainly is not). For Aunt Celine, it is the presence of *any* bathing suit that presents a problem. Age, vanity, and modesty aside, all the ladies of Lake Wecausett —especially Genette ladies—swim naked at dawn. This has always been the way. Especially today. For Celine's last swim. Still, tradition or not, Nan cannot bring herself to strip naked before her decrepit great-aunt. She hides her suit beneath a buttoned-up oxford and cutoffs.

Nan has been to Swimmers' Rock only once, five years ago, to join the dawn swim with her mother. She had been on the verge then. Her body, her life, all like a bud so full it would pop open at the slightest pressure. Nan had had errant hairs and plum-sized breasts and the monthly shame that her mother would only refer to as *the curse*, leaving a daisy-festooned pamphlet on her bedside table.

That time, they had arrived at dawn, along with two of Celine's bridge friends: one with hair dyed orange, the other dyed blue. A fog hid the opposite shore. Like Celine, these ladies bundled against the chill in thick terry-cloth robes. Nan wore only a nightie and her arms and chest goose-pimpled from the combination of chill and excitement. *Did you see the new boy driving the ferry? I'll ride any time he's driving.* The old ladies laughed at their raunchy comedy routine.

Nan couldn't stop staring at all the female bodies—all the damage done by babies and years. Her Aunt Celine's body, like those of her friends, was bone and hanging flesh. Breasts like stones in stockings swung from her shoulders. Her flat, dimpled buttocks were like gray elephant's hide. And Alice's nakedness was a shock to Nan, too. Before that moment, all Nan had known of her mother's body she had deduced from the vaguely terrifying undergarments drying in the basement, supported and boned things, as if Alice's body were made of Play-Doh and held its shape only through substructure. In reality, Alice was slight and willowy. A tremulous, baby wren of a person. More bone than clay.

The old women shimmied into the cold water like otters and gave Nan's body the twice over. Celine's blue-haired friend told Nan that her own breasts were once so pert: *bounced like rubber balls, but my babies shriveled them up.* Miss Orange Hair told Nan, *You'll have more boyfriends than you can handle.*

Their cackles echoed across the still water, broadcasting Nan's shame.

"You're just jealous, you old crones," Celine said, meaning it but laughing, too. Nan had been grateful for an ally. Grateful to be able to laugh. Alice, facing away, didn't laugh or say anything at all.

Five Pines is awash in the sepia of early morning. Nan's mother lies in wait for her in the living room, pouncing as soon as Nan emerges from her bedroom.

"There's a ton to get done today before we bring Celine over to St. Anne's," says Alice. Even with a bandanna tied over her bob and wearing yellow rubber gloves, Alice would never be mistaken for a maid. Not to mention that there are no signs that she has been doing any actual work. She hasn't bothered with accessories for her show: no sponge, no Clorox, no rags.

Nan has learned to read her mother's mood by looking at her eyebrows. Alice has overplucked them for years and now must pencil them back in each morning. If the brows are drawn high, Alice is feeling curious. Arched means sexy. Flat is anxious. Today the situation is bad enough that Alice has drawn nothing at all. Nan knows better than to argue with blank brows when Alice says, "I'm thinking it would be better if I stayed here to get Celine's things ready. You take her swimming. I don't think I can pack with her underfoot."

Swimming—even in the glacial lake—is better than packing up Celine's paltry possessions into some cracked, leather valise. Still, Nan flops onto the red velvet sofa that dominates the mammoth living room. With its carved legs and tufted, tasseled pillows, the sofa was once a regal throne in the Victorian mansion of Nan's great-great-grandparents. In any other setting, it would look like a bordello cast-off. Fifty years at the camp have faded the velvet from cabernet red to the tawny orange of cough syrup. The velvet has bald patches and, even worse, patches where the nap is stiff with unidentified, hardened filth. Celine spends her days on the behemoth, stroking it with affection, and leaving her old-lady residue of Vicks VapoRub and grease from last night's fried chicken. Nan loves this decaying piece of decadence, though she avoids the stiff patches. Alice refuses to sit on the vile thing altogether.

Alice says, "Besides, she likes you better." She tucks a hair beneath her bandanna. Then she says in her mothering tone of voice, "Eat before you go. Use up the milk."

Without looking, Nan knows that Alice has pulled all the muscles of her face into a pucker. Even her missing eyebrows are frowning. Nan sighs. Alice disappears into the kitchen and returns with a tray of coffee and toast.

Nan says, "Do I have to feed her?" She would use the same tone for picking up doggy doo.

"Be a good girl," says Alice.

Out on the porch, Nan says to Celine, "Do you want milk in your tea? Or lemon?"

Celine looks at Nan and then at the creamer.

"She isn't listening again," says Nan to her mother.

"Just give her milk then." Alice sighs to remind Nan that there are bigger things to worry about.

Alice insists on pretending that Celine's time at St. Anne's will only be a vacation of sorts. Something to do in the off-season. Like heading to Florida. Nan can't tell if this is to assuage Alice's guilt or to keep Celine sedate for admission day, like telling a child that a tetanus shot won't hurt. If it's the latter, Alice is failing; Celine knows the score. Yesterday she said that no one would lock her up without a fight.

Alice had said, "I'd have thought you'd be excited to spend some time with Uncle Ted. I had to pull some strings to get you in, you know."

At the mention of Ted's name, Celine quieted. "That goddamned fool left me here to rot." Celine cried noiselessly: water seeping from her eyes and nose and mouth.

This morning everything about Celine is slack. Her bathrobe gapes open, displaying her mottled breastbone; her dentures slip and click after each sloppy, open-mouthed swallow, and her eyes and mouth droop. Overnight she has developed a talcum-powder-and-ammonia smell, like a baby in need of a change. A wet toast crumb splats onto Nan's arm. She flashes her mother a look of revulsion.

Across the lake, they can just barely see Stanley Merrill hoisting an oversized flag up his flagpole. The self-proclaimed mayor of Lake Wecausett.

Alice says to Celine, "So, how's Mayor Merrill holding up?"

Her chipper query fades unanswered into Celine's crunching. When the pause has been long enough that Alice's comment seems dead, Celine says, "He's coming for drinks tonight. With Betty and the baby. You better treat him with some manners, Chickie. Don't be such a damned snob this time."

Alice replies, in a loud and well-enunciated voice that does nothing to disguise her irritation, "Aunt Celine? It's me, Alice. Chickie died a long time ago. I'm her daughter. Remember?"

BRIGHT WHITE FLAGPOLES DOT the edge of Lake Wecausett like giant picket-fence posts. It is late enough in the morning for most of the flags to be up. Even the ferry boys have remembered to raise their huge Stars and Stripes. In a couple of hours, they'll start carting tourists from the highway to The Shack to buy ice cream and burgers and postcards curled with humidity. Stanley Merrill, in his polished runabout, hoists a dozen flags for camp owners who otherwise wouldn't bother. Usually Stanley stops at Celine's dock, too, but he is respecting her privacy. He knows Alice has come. He knows why, too. He called Alice for her help. Still, for the last five mornings he has felt a keen ache at the sight of Celine's bare flagpole.

Stanley is eighty-five, but the only obvious indicators of his age are his bald head with its monk's fringe of gray hair that he hides beneath a Yankees' cap, and the hump growing between his shoulder blades. The combination gives him the look of a furtive chipmunk. Back in the fifties, Stanley built his own A-frame on the lake with help and enthusiasm from his wife Betty. When it was done, he began working as a carpenter for the great camps, those wooden behemoths in constant need of repair. Come winter, when all the camp owners headed back to the city, he kept an eye on things. Still does. His regular, well-to-do customers pay for his watchful eye; those with modest A-frames and log cabins on his side of the lake do not. He looks after them just the same. Stanley looks after Five Pines, too, though Celine would never pay him a dime. Not that he would take it if she tried.

The Genettes had been the first wealthy people Stanley had ever met. The day they interviewed him to work at their camp, they picked him up in a glossy wooden runabout. Ted drove absentmindedly while Celine lounged on the white leather cushions in the stern. Stanley had wanted nothing more than to drive that boat. No, he *had* wanted more than that. He wanted to own it. He wanted to be Ted Genette—so what if he was shell-shocked—driving around the lake like a king in his slick, teak chariot with its chrome wheel.

Ted was a small man but athletic. He must have been in his early forties already, but his stature and freckles made him seem much younger. He didn't seem at all crazy, despite the rumors, only a bit quiet. That and the fact that he couldn't seem to make eye contact. He sat in his captain's chair, idling the engine while Celine made the introductions.

Celine was fair-haired like her brother but already bronzed just a month into summer. She had deep-set eyes, brown, the color of loam and flecked with gold. They reminded Stanley of the Wecausett water at sundown and, embarrassed by such a girlish thought, he blushed frantically and looked at his feet.

Celine wore a crisp, white shirt knotted at her ribcage above high-waisted pedal pushers. As she climbed back, Stanley noticed that her stomach and back were the same honey-baked color as her face and arms. She was as evenly toasted as a marshmallow.

He tripped on the boarding ladder and reached for something to steady himself, landing on Ted's shoulder. Ted flinched.

"Teddy, be nice," scolded Celine. She winked at Stanley. "Word has it you're just the man for our job."

ALICE FINDS VERY LITTLE of Celine's belongings worth packing. Her underwear and nightgowns are pilled, saggy, and gray as gruel. She tosses in a few of the dozens of framed photos on Celine's dresser: Grandmother and Grandfather Genette's wedding day, Ted as an officer, a smirking threesome of young Ted, Celine, and baby Chickie on the dock. The only color picture is a Polaroid of Ted in a plastic lawn chair on the porch, staring off. It's the only way Alice has ever known her uncle. The War omnipresent in his mind. If he wasn't sitting and staring, Uncle Ted was up in his second floor bedroom, or chauffeuring Celine and her pals, a task he performed like a grateful employee. A middle-aged monolith of a man. Damaged. Irreparable. Alice tucks in a snapshot of her and Nan from her own wallet, in case Celine needs help remembering who they are.

Alice feels little kinship with Five Pines. Chickie stopped bringing her for summers when she was still young, right after Ted and Celine's winterization hid the woody interior and all its grand memories under layers of wallboard, asbestos, carpet, and linoleum. Things had chilled between the sisters after that.

Alice can't believe it has fallen to her to take care of Celine. That there's no one else left. She's the one left picking up the pieces. It is one thing to take care of your own mother, but Celine? Celine who said only stupid women have children. Celine who told Alice on her wedding day—without an ounce of alcohol in her—that she was spoiled just like Chickie. Just looking for all the trimmings.

Ted's room looks just as it did when he moved to St. Anne's, as it always has. Long ago someone (could it possibly be Celine?) had taken the time to hang a boyish collection of banners and trophies and war memorabilia. On his desk by the window is a massive pair of binoculars. Alice sits at the desk and looks across the lake with them. The view from here is better than the floor below. The binoculars are powerful. Alice watches the boys on the ferry horsing around and Stanley Merrill on his dock looking across the lake with his own binoculars. Alice tries to spot Nan and Celine but even from up here the pine trees block Swimmers' Rock.

Alice sifts through Ted's things with no compunction. Yellowed news clippings on his bulletin board record every tragic event that happened on the lake in his tenure. You'd never guess such a hermit crab of a person was paying attention to all the news. The bad news. Chickie's obituary. An older one for Betty Merrill. A cottage burns down: two dead. Boat sinks: pilot intoxicated. Alice feels the morbidity on her fingertips like chalkdust.

POST-BREAKFAST CELINE IS A different person altogether. Like a secret twin, this new Celine lives in Celine's room and vaguely resembles her but wears smart plaid Bermuda shorts and pale pink lipstick and a straw hat. New Celine says, "We're late for our swim. We've already missed the others. If there *were* any others today. It's a dying tradition."

Swimmers' Rock, despite its name, is the only sandy part of the lakeshore. Each spring the town dumps a boatload of sand, and Stanley Merrill rakes it out as a public service. A tremendous, flat boulder takes up a quarter of the beach. A perfect island for climbing, lounging, and drying towels. A fifty-foot dock stretches into the lake with a fleet of communal boats tied to rings along one side.

Celine sheds her clothes with surprising speed and grace. Her body is every bit as decrepit as Nan remembers. Only a little more bone, a little less flesh. A little more curve to her tired spine, a little less blush to her skin.

When Nan has finally stripped off her own shorts and T-shirt, Celine says, "Christ Almighty, what is that thing you're wearing?"

"My bathing suit," says Nan.

"You are a Genette no matter what that father of yours says. Strip down, girl."

Nan doesn't mention that her father is two years dead: heart attack. She doesn't try to defend herself like she might if Alice were there. She *does* glance around, though. The last time she joined the ladies of the lake, it hadn't been so late in the morning, so fog-free, so *awake*. The sky hasn't a trace of daybreak pink, just the cloudless blue that lets the sun bake the tops of Nan and Celine's heads.

Celine cautiously makes her way to the lake's edge, having lost the surefootedness of five years earlier, but once afloat seems rejuvenated. She bobs in the copper water, her arms gently treading. Her wet hair is translucent, exposing her rosy scalp. She openly stares at a now-naked Nan.

Everything private about Nan begins to feel bigger, brighter, illuminated with neon. Her breasts are massive water balloons with nipples like red grapes, her pubic hair a full skein of frizzled black yarn. Celine watches her walk down the dock. Nan walks faster then, to speed up this horrible parade, and then she is running. At the end of the dock, she hurls herself off, arms and legs akimbo, hair blown back. For a moment, she is resplendent and triumphant, like Icarus. *Go ahead, Celine, look.*

Nan enters the water in a jumble, with no pointed toes or streamlined legs. The water slaps hard against the back of her thighs and spanks her bottom. A frigid blast rushes inside her, freezing up everything that should be sacrosanct and hygienically sealed. She shivers. And everything—the follicles of her hairs, her nipples, her very pores—feels the arctic caress. The lake water, full of decaying pine, is as soft as talcum powder beneath its chill, and Nan likes sliding through it, like fresh linen sheets on a January night. When she surfaces, she hears Celine yell, "Bloody hell!"

In this moment, Nan likes this old lady. Their shared nakedness. Celine's raunchy language that Nan wishes she had the nerve to use. Nan smiles at Celine in triumph, but Celine's mouth is set sideways across her face like a slit. Nan's leap now feels foolish. Gloating. She is a scene-stealer. She slows the movement of her arms to make herself seem less alive.

Celine says, "Sure, you can fly, girly. But can you swim?"

CELINE DOESN'T LIKE WHEN Betty Merrill flaunts herself. Even with a two-year-old baby at home, Betty has the body of a teenager. Of course, she *does* ship that child off to her mother with alarming frequency. Maybe motherhood hasn't really gotten its claws into her yet. Celine knows a thing or two about mothering from the last decade with Teddy. It's true, it's aged her, but she doesn't mind. So no tennis lessons or golf, like Chickie has. It's her choice. Stanley says it's different with a real baby. Things happen. In the mind. *It's taken its toll on Betty. She's fragile, Celine.* But when Betty shows off like this, leaping into the air like some spastic duck, it's all Celine can do not to tell her what's what. Stanley and Celine have talked it out. Plans have been made. Celine won't wait much longer.

Betty looks nimble enough today. Her breasts are all bounce and jiggle. Certainly took her time getting in the water, too. Making sure Ted and Stanley got a good look with the binoculars. Celine's been watching Betty flirt with Ted. Now who's the fragile one? Betty brings him root beer floats from The Shack at the end of her shift. Pretends she's interested in whatever he dredges up about the war. She tells Celine, through that pinched nose of hers, that it's good how he talks to her. *Did you see him laugh today, Celine? I think he's improving quite impressively.* Celine can tell Betty's doing her best to sound smart.

When Betty surfaces, still smiling from her jump, Celine says, "Sure, you can fly, girly. But can you swim?"

Betty may be fifteen years her junior, but Celine knows of no woman (and hardly any men) who can swim faster than she can. Certainly not some Brooklyn floozy like Betty. Celine moves through the water as if she were born in it. Which, really, she was.

CELINE'S BREASTSTROKE IS A quiet, froggy motion that moves her in tiny, patient increments across the lake. Nan had expected something better than this. Some shocking reservoir of youth loosened in Celine by the old familiar routine. Like her morning renewals. But Celine swims like the old turtle she is. Nan treads water, waiting for Celine to be done, like waiting for a dog to do its business. Her feet dangle down to where the water is dramatically cooler. With each kick, Nan stirs a frigid eddy, water that feels thick and black like congealed ink. She lets herself sink a little lower on each stroke, imagining a dangerous vortex sucking her down, down, down. When Nan's toes scrape against the muck of the bottom, she bolts to the surface. No one sees her silliness. There is only Celine, now a hundred yards offshore, still inching forward.

"Celine," Nan calls. If the old woman hears, she doesn't respond.

"Seriously, Celine. It's time to get out." Nan's petulant voice carries across the still morning the way a metallic clang moves through water, inexplicably resonant. *Goddamn it, Celine. Turn around.*

Stroke, stroke, stroke, look. And each time Nan looks, Celine seems to have drifted farther to the right. Nan blames the old woman for not being able to swim in a straight line.

Nan swims until her shoulders ache and her heart does its ba-BUMP, ba-BUMP. Twice she treads water to catch her breath. Celine keeps the same pace. *Damn it, Celine. Damn it. Damn it.* Nan cannot get enough air into her lungs.

BETTY IS GAINING ON her. This won't do. Celine switches to her front crawl. She is unbeatable with this stroke. Betty is close now, and she is yelling at Celine. Expecting Celine to give up. But they are almost at the Merrills' dock, and Celine will be damned if she hasn't earned her victory moment.

On her next upstroke, Betty grabs Celine's arm, and Celine instantly takes in water and gags. She sinks a few inches, takes in another swig. Celine grabs at the surface for traction in a frenzied splashing.

"I'm right here, Celine. Hold on," says Betty.

Hold on? She can damned well hold on. Celine slaps at Betty and her helpful hands. She tries for a second slap but her arms feel leaden, and her hands land heavily on Betty's shoulders. Like exhausted boxers clinging to each other, they sink a foot below the surface. Down there, the orange water is calm. And quiet. *It's okay. Okay. Let go. Let. Go.* And Betty does. And Celine does, too, as if it has been willed on her. Betty sinks lower, down where the water turns from orange to rust. Celine watches her go. In the copper murk, Betty seems to be smiling. Victorious. Then a stomach cramp jackknifes Celine's body. A sucker-punch. All her air escapes in one large bubble, and she greedily gulps, sucking water into her lungs.

STANLEY MERRILL FOCUSES HIS binoculars on the slowly moving pink head. Usually the swimming women come earlier, in a group, if they come at all now. He watches the head a little longer until he recognizes it as Celine. *What the devil are you up to now?* Stanley settles himself onto the transom of his motorboat to watch the proceedings. Celine moves slowly, even for a patient man like Stanley.

He hasn't spoken to her much lately. Sure, he keeps an eye on her, but mostly he keeps his distance. Stopping by once a week to be neighborly. Calling her niece about the state of affairs with Celine—well, that was just the humane thing to do. He *had* found Celine wandering the lake path looking for Ted. Still taking care of him. Even now. Wasted her whole life on that empty-shell man. But she wouldn't listen. Not Celine. Lord knows he had tried.

Celine has switched to a crawl, and Stanley spots a second person, close behind, swimming in a drunken, serpentine path.

Celine and Betty used to swim the lake almost every day. Like sirens swimming over to tempt him. He never tired of it. *Stanley,* Celine would call out, all flirty. *Your bevy has arrived.* And Stanley always pretended he hadn't been waiting, watching. But he hadn't been watching closely enough. Hadn't been there the one time it mattered. *Where were you?* Celine had screamed. *She sank. Where were you?* He was with the baby. The baby had cried.

By the time the other swimmer finally reaches Celine, they are only a hundred feet from where Stanley sits. Water splashes around them like trout in a net. Stanley and his boat are well-equipped for such emergencies.

"Not me," growls Celine when he gets close. "Her. Get her."

Once both women are safely onboard, Stanley says to the stranger, "Are you okay?" She isn't much more than a girl, he sees now. Stanley tries not to linger on her breasts and curves, though he rubs her back as she bends forward gagging.

"I'm fine," she says. Her voice is raspy.

"You okay, Celine?"

Celine nods but says nothing.

Stanley risks putting his hand on the girl's back again. He rubs her cool, knobby spine. The girl moves away from his touch and crosses her arms over her breasts.

"She said she was fine," says Celine. "Stop leering and get us some towels."

"I knew you couldn't swim," says Celine to the girl.

"Me? I was trying to save you."

"Save me? From what? You almost killed me."

"You almost killed *yourself*."

Stanley stiffens, as he does anytime anyone mentions suicide.

Celine shuts her mouth and looks out across the lake toward Five Pines.

The girl grabs the frayed brown towels Stanley proffers. She tosses one to Celine, who lets it lie in her lap. The girl covers herself, whipping the towel around her torso, tossing her long hair out of the way, in a motion as smooth as a bird pivoting in flight. How long has it been since Stanley saw a woman move like that? The girl glares at him. He knows he must seem the dirty old man, but he can't stop. The ache bores through him, through his throat, and his stomach and his testicles, all the way to his boney toes.

"You must be related," he says. "You look just like a young Celine."

The girl tightens her towel. "I'm her great-niece," she says. He can tell she finds him repulsive.

Stanley nods at this information.

"Well, looks like you two could use a ride back across," Stanley says.

"You're a cocksucker, Stanley Merrill," Celine says.

The words settle around the boat like cold dew. Stanley would have predicted anything other than this. Gratitude. Nostalgia. She's disoriented, of course. Senile. Confused. Still, she used his name. She looked him in the eye. The girl looks down at her feet. Even though she hides it, he can see her smug smile.

Alice pulls into the parking lot of St. Anne's and breathes deep. Nan gives her an encouraging smile. Celine has been ranting nonstop for the better part of three hours, ever since Stanley Merrill dropped her and Nan off, half-naked, at their dock. Alice wills a couple of nice orderlies to appear, to whisk Celine away without a fuss. But the doors to St. Anne's don't open.

"Here we are, Aunt Celine. Let's go check on Ted, shall we?"

Celine is reaching panic. "Chickie, you've got to believe me. It wasn't my fault. Betty didn't want my help."

"It's okay," says Alice, as she already has two dozen times. "I believe you. Everyone believes you. Now let's just head inside, okay?"

"No. No. No. Stanley doesn't believe me. You've got to talk to him."

"Listen, Mr. Merrill is fine. He dropped you off. You've had a fright. But you're fine. Nan's fine." Alice turns off the engine and opens her door to a blast of hot air. Away from the lake, the day is sweltering.

"It wasn't my fault," repeats Celine. "You know I wouldn't do something like that. Talk to him."

Alice steps out of the car and stands by the open door. Nan doesn't move. She's been useless since the swim. Maybe the accident was worse than Alice had thought. Mr. Merrill had said only, "Looks like the ladies went a little too far. Good thing I was there."

Alice leans back into the open car. "Nan, can you help me out here? Please?" Alice opens Celine's door and unlocks her seat belt. Celine grabs her sleeve with a gnarled hand. Inches away, Alice must look straight into her aunt's eyes. They are cloudy brown and wet with emotion. They hide in the hollows of her eye-sockets, unprotected by eyelashes or brows. Utterly exposed.

Celine lowers her voice, "Please, Chickie. Do this for me. I can't lose him."

Chickie never got old. She died when she was Alice's age, but in the end she looked nearly as old as Celine does now. Chickie had wanted things from Alice, too. Small comforts Alice could not provide. Alice pushes Celine's hand away, stands up, smoothes her blouse and walks to the doors. There are supposed to be people here to help.

Nan retrieves Celine's sad little suitcase from the trunk. "Let's go," she says to Celine.

Celine calls after Alice, "Not everyone got to run off with Mr. Right. Waltz away in that goddamned country-club life. Someone had to watch Teddy. Didn't they? Wasn't you, was it? You always had it easy, Chickie."

Easy? Alice thinks of her withering mother with the tubes and IV drips and her father pretending to be too busy to leave the office. *Easy.*

She walks back to Celine and takes her firmly by the shoulders.

"Mom!" says Nan. "Leave her alone."

"I am *not* Chickie. I am Alice. Chickie's dead. It's over, you crazy fool."

THE RIDE BACK TO Boston is quiet. Nan drives and Alice sleeps. Then Alice drives and Nan sleeps. They stop in a diner for coffee. Nan is hungry again. She orders pie. Alice looks at the congealed cherries with disgust.

"Pie's about the worst possible thing for your figure, you know."

"She wanted to die, Mom. I saw it on her face."

"Don't be ridiculous. You can't be suicidal when you don't know what year it is."

"You weren't there. And you should have heard her with Mr. Merrill."

"Well, I wasn't there. But I do know she's a senile old woman who can't be taken seriously. You'll understand better when you're older."

"When *you're* the senile old woman, you mean?"

By February, Stanley Merrill has grown tired of his patrols. What was novel in December—spotting the first cardinal in the snow, the holy sensation of gliding across the middle of a lake—has grown mundane. It does every year. This morning he waits until after his second cup of coffee before strapping on his skis.

Stanley's long parallel tracks are the only sign of human life on Wecausett. This no longer feels magical but depressing. His breathing has become more ragged. He will call Dr. Alter when he gets home, if the phone line is working.

A gust cuts across the lake and rattles the ice-coated branches. They tinkle like the wind chimes Betty used to make out of translucent shells she found on their trips to Nova Scotia. How many years has it been since he last thought of those things? His mind dredges up lost trivia in little sludgy bits every day now.

At Swimmers' Rock, he stops to rest. He leans against the boulder where the ladies dry their towels. Behind him, hidden in the icy pines, are sections of the communal dock, stacked and covered in tarps, and snow-shrouded, overturned hulls like burial mounds.

He pulls a thermos from his backpack. It is army grade and was a Christmas gift from his son, Neil. Stanley hasn't seen Neil in three—no, four—years. But packages arrive on his birthday and Christmas. He calls, too, on the day Betty died, though neither of them really has much to say then. Stanley sips his still-hot cup of coffee and thinks with satisfaction of the good character of the boy. Man. The coffee's hot bitterness thaws his toes. He makes good coffee. A simple skill to be proud of.

Stanley thinks about Celine's grand-niece. She has become his favorite distraction this winter. He pictures her cradling her breasts like fragile fruit against her chest. He thinks of the exposed dimple of her navel. Everything he wasn't supposed to see. He enjoys the fact that he can still get hard just thinking about this succulent thing. It doesn't last, though. Every time he thinks of the girl, he will eventually hear Celine's voice. And see the girl laughing. Just rescued from drowning— both of them—and laughing at him. Stanley feels sullied. Unappreciated. But tomorrow he will conjure her again, to his beach, or his boat, or the dock: a nymph, beckoning him. Like Celine used to. He is not dead yet.

It's odd that he never meditates on how things used to be with Celine. It's not because they aren't good memories for him but because Celine is still here, has *always* been here. Only the people who leave him seem to lodge in the net of his memory. Betty. Neil. With Celine, it's different. Stanley has stayed in his A-frame and she in her camp, following the same rituals, the same seasons, year-on-year. The years wrap around him, one on top of the other, like translucent layers of wet tissue paper. Only when Celine called him that disgusting word did he realize just how far they have evolved from their old intimacy. How he wishes he could sink backward in time to when Celine was waiting for him to take her around the shoulder, to sneak her away to his boat, or out to the gazebo, back when it still had a view of the stars.

At the edge of the Genettes' property, Stanley spots a raw and jagged tree trunk. Ice storms snap pines. Especially if you don't cull the weak trees. You have to take care of your property if you want it to last.

Stanley removes his skis and trudges through the snow to the severed trunk. The rest of the tree, fifty feet—no, more— has landed on the roof of Five Pines. Plywood and shingles and tarpaper jut skyward like an open wound. Stanley sees the attic detritus, all those things stored away for safekeeping now at the mercy of an Adirondack winter. He sees shattered stair banisters and the tattered, blue-striped wallpaper of Ted's bedroom. As intimate as underpants.

Stanley skis home faster than normal, his arms and legs flapping and gliding. His hip flexors aching. Then his triceps. His tracks unspool behind him in a straight line from Five Pines toward home. He suspects he is having a heart attack. Or maybe not. He takes aspirin and lies very still. Stanley tells himself he will call St. Anne's and the Fire Department and Dr. Alter. Somewhere, too, he still has Alice's phone number from when he called about Celine. Stanley imagines the girl answering for her mother in her low, laughing voice.

That night, in the dark, Stanley pictures Five Pines before the tree severed it. A rich man's woody retreat gone sour. With bookshelves loaded with moldy books and French doors too swollen to close. Too much furniture. What had he once coveted about it? Certainly not that obscene red sofa. Celine had joked about it back in the days of cocktails and bridge. She exhaled her smoke steadily as she said the word: *whorehouse*. Ted, Stanley, and Betty had laughed at her naughtiness. And then Stanley had caught Celine's eye above their collective laughter.

It RAINS MOST OF April. Torrential, diluvial rain. Stanley Merrill dreams that the red sofa exposed to the weather is filling up with water, swelling like a sponge. Like some inflamed bodily organ. In his three A.M. panic, he promises he will call in the morning. He has promised this to himself every night since it happened. It is his caretaker's duty to report the damage. And then morning comes and he makes coffee instead. Maybe he'll call later. But, really, what can you say after so much time has passed?

Wisteria

Fiona wonders how it is possible that she has lost her son, her husband, her house, and even her wisteria. One by one over the last sixteen years these cornerstones of her adult life have been taken away. She is now unmoored. Untethered. Adrift. So many words she can think of, but none capture the terror she feels at this unwanted emancipation. Per the realtor's instructions, Fiona broom-sweeps the rooms, switches off the lights, leaves the keys on the kitchen counter, and turns the lock on her way out. The temperature has dropped at least ten degrees over the course of the afternoon, and Fiona tightens her wrap against the December wind. The blue sky doesn't hint at the storm forecast she saw on the morning news. Fiona refuses to look back. She will not let her final moment of ownership be one of remorse, preferring instead to imagine the house as it had looked every spring, burgeoning with fragrant lavender clumps. For those two weeks, the mammoth white antique, pillared and balconied like a Georgian plantation grafted onto New England soil, was the prettiest house in a town full of pretty houses. Fiona aches to return to the familiar rooms just one last time. The urge works its way up from her small feet, but she knows it is an impulse best ignored. Instead, Fiona walks straight-spined to a waiting station wagon loaded with the detritus of more than four decades.

The other homeowners on Main Street have fully decked the halls. Swags and wreathes on doors and porch railings and picket fences, little white lights on the evergreens, and electric candles in every window. Fiona has lived in this secure and serene place for most of her adult life, but Old Stonington always was Nick's town. Every inch known to him and every inch of him known to it. Had it not been for Nick's inheritance, they would never have been able to afford to stay. They would have had to drop down a few rungs, to Black Brook or Richmond, and how might things have turned out differently for them if they had? But Fiona had long ago embraced this safe life with its calming predictability, devoted to her gardening, to her son Sully, and to Nick.

Soon after they moved to town, Fiona had dragged Nick to endless charity functions, hoping to make friends. Nick said he'd had plenty of time to pick the friends he wanted in Old Stonington, and there was good reason these people weren't among them. But Fiona couldn't get comfortable with Nick's set, men who had grown up in town and never left. They taught shop or English at the private school they had all attended—Nick included. They were the sons of more successful fathers, or, in Sully's case, the grandsons, since Nick and Fiona certainly couldn't have afforded the academy without her in-laws' help. And then there were the practical men who ran the luncheonette and the pharmacy. There was a probate judge and a dentist. But Fiona had tried to cultivate a different social circle among the mothers of Sully's friends. Women who chaired the Garden Club or held seats on the Historic District Commission or ran the academy's Parents' Association. These friendships sparked and then fizzled, but even now Fiona continues to attend their events, pleasantly positioned off to the side. She knows she is an extra in Old Stonington's social scene, and as much as she had once hoped for a substantial role, it still is better to have a bit part than nothing.

On Friday, June 25, 1999, not long after sunrise, Fiona had been perched on her front-porch steps, nursing a hangover headache, when Officer Jimmy Mino parked his cruiser on the street, hitched up his trousers, and lumbered up her walk. She thought, as she always did when she saw him, that his bulk must keep him from effectively performing his job. But other than shutting down the occasional kegger at the reservoir or escorting some poor demented senior citizen back to Standish Arms, there wasn't much to be done in Old Stonington that required an exertion of energy. Wasn't that why everyone paid such outrageous taxes? As an insurance policy against tragedy, disappointment, and failure.

Fiona had known Jimmy Mino since the high school summers he had worked construction with Sully, and she had watched his waistline increase inch by inch over the intervening decade. His father was a town cop, too. Sully and his drama-club friends used to call the older man The Minotaur because of his enormous bulky body and his notoriously bad temper. They'd snort and brandish faux horns when Mino Sr. swaggered through town. But whatever mean things lived inside The Minotaur, his son hadn't inherited any of them. Sure, Jimmy was a bit daft and eternally apologetic—Fiona could picture him pausing to ask permission before slapping on handcuffs—but his congeniality made him a town favorite.

"Awful early for you to be out and about, isn't it?" she asked.

The horror in Jimmy Mino's face at her question jolted Fiona to the recognition that, yes, indeed, it was an ungodly hour—a frightening hour—for a police officer, even gentle Jimmy Mino, to be coming to her door.

Jimmy squinted up to the second floor balcony as if he hoped to see Nick surveying his property from there.

"Mr. Faydah home, too?"

The truth was Fiona didn't know exactly where Nick had gone. He had slept on the sofa, something that had been happening more often than not. He stayed up later than she did and liked to let some late-night comedian lull him to sleep. And the night before who knew how late it had been when he succumbed? By the time Fiona had come down this morning for aspirin and tea, Nick and Sully were both gone: two cars, no notes.

"He's out fishing with the Judge," she said.

It was a polite lie. The kind her mother used to call a *You bloody well shouldn't have asked me in the first place* fib. Fiona pulled a few petals from the nearest cluster of wisteria. She crushed them between her thumb and forefinger to intensify their scent. Her mother had always wanted wisteria at their cottage, but the soil there wouldn't let it take root, and each attempt died in the first few years before ever managing to flower. The petals' purple moistness smeared against Fiona's fingertips, and she hoped that if she didn't look up, Jimmy Mino would head back to his cruiser and the police station and get busy on whatever it was he usually did at this private hour.

Instead, Jimmy doffed his hat and stuck it into his armpit. He shifted his feet into formal military stance, like his round body might need a sturdier foundation for what he was about to say. He cleared his throat twice.

"Go ahead then," said Fiona.

"Sully's dead."

With such a ridiculously blunt delivery, Fiona might have thought for a moment that it was a joke. The kind of joke, in fact, that Sully and his friends would have found hilarious. But this was Jimmy Mino.

"There was a car accident. Out by the reservoir. About two hours ago. We got an ambulance crew there in ten minutes, but it was too late."

His dreaded speech completed, Jimmy relaxed his body. When he spoke again, his voice cracked, "I'm so sorry, Mrs. Faydah. Oh my God, I'm so, so sorry."

Fiona stood up then. This soft face, pinched with its crying, repulsed her. She backed across the wide porch. There, in the shadows, none of this was happening. She backed all the way to the screen door, wisteria petals slipping from her fist and leaving a trail like miniature baby footprints on the black porch boards. Jimmy came up the steps then, an arm outstretched, and Fiona felt a panic to avoid his touching her. She swung open the screen door, slamming it shut before lethargic Jimmy could get there.

Locked in the downstairs bathroom, Fiona wretched into the toilet. Out came every ounce of champagne and lo mein from the night before, along with this morning's therapeutic tea and toast. Then came every molecule of acid that lives inside a gut, and when she had nothing left, she heaved rancid air. Fiona lay then on the cool tile floor, coiled around the toilet, and rocked her shivering self. Later and for weeks, months, years even, tears would leak from her eyes without warning, embarrassingly constant evidence of the grief she harbored, but she didn't cry that morning in the bathroom, not a tear, not a sob. When the clock in the hall chimed the hour, Jimmy Mino called out tentatively: "Mrs. Faydah? Hello? I think maybe we need to talk a little more."

Fiona scrubbed her face raw with the pumice soap she used after gardening and clawed her lank hair into a severe little bun. For a woman who usually looked a decade younger than her fifty-four years, the last ten minutes had made up the suspended time. When she looked in the mirror, the reality of what was happening doubled back on her. She gripped the sink and another wave of nausea moved through her.

"Right," said Fiona when she was back in the hall, face to face with Jimmy, the screen door's wire mesh safely between them. He told her that Sully was at the hospital. He didn't say *the remains* or *the body* or, God forbid, *the corpse*, just that when Nick got home they should come straight to the hospital.

He didn't say *the morgue*, either, and Fiona was glad for his squeamishness.

When Jimmy stopped repeating himself, Fiona nodded her head a few times too many.

"You want me to go get Mr. Faydah? I can do that, no problem. I know just the spot they've been fishing."

And Fiona's little lie glared at her: white, shiny, and hot like a blister.

"Don't. Please. He'll be home soon. Then we'll come down. Like you said."

Jimmy looked forlorn the way he used to when peddling raffle tickets door-to-door for the Booster Club back in high school.

"You can leave now," said Fiona.

"Well, I don't know. How about I get one of the neighbors? Mrs. Stanton?"

"No," said Fiona a little loudly, and Jimmy smarted.

The thought that one of those pecking hens should stand as witness to her agony repulsed Fiona. This pain would be her own.

"I mean, you should go. It's all right. Nick will be here soon."

Jimmy cocked his head to the side, and Fiona could see him deciding about her, about her bright dry eyes, about his responsibility to this strange, shocked woman, about what should happen next.

Fiona and Nick didn't talk about Sully's death. Sure, they handled the details of the service. The flowers were imported calla lilies, and Sully wore the suit Fiona had gotten him as a college-graduation present. The undertaker tried, but failed, to capture Sully's early summer complexion, the glow of youth translated under his hand into a horrid Tang orange. And Sully's playful peroxide blond hair seemed grotesque. At First Congregational, Reverend Moore spoke eloquently of Sully's rambunctious high-school years and his promising career as an actor. Donations were made, by Nick's decision, to the Actors' Guild AIDS Fund, and Fiona had been too numb to object. But not once did either mention how much champagne Sully had had to drink that night with Fiona and Nick, and how much of whatever else he might have had after Fiona had gone to bed. Neither mentioned the throngs of young men at the funeral—friends from New York, friends from the theater—one particularly bereaved. Hugo was his name. He and Sully had been together for nearly two years. *I'm Hugo*, he had said when he shook Fiona's hand with both of his own, as if surely she must have long been waiting to put a face to this name. As if in other circumstances she would have smiled and said, *Ah, at last, it's the famous Hugo!* Fiona listened politely as this same person, really not much more than a teenager, described his loss—her loss, Fiona thought— to the gathered crowd, quoting Whitman. Fiona had watched Nick shake this Hugo's hand. Thanking him for the kind words. Reaching with his other hand to Hugo's shoulder to reinforce the sentiment. Fiona hoped only that he would leave before the reception. That she would never have to see his lively, boyish face again.

It occurs to Fiona that nowadays Hugo and Sully could have gotten married. She wonders if they would have stuck together all these years. She might even have had a grandchild. There's a lesbian couple that comes to Starbucks with an infant they adopted from somewhere in South America. It amazes Fiona how different things are today from 1999, not to mention when she was girl in Surrey.

After Fiona had seen to it that every funeral guest was paired off with a suitable conversational partner and that the caterers were doing all she had asked, she disappeared up the kitchen stairs to her bedroom, shrouded as it was by the wisteria even on that bright June day. She lay down on the bed and crushed a pillow to her chest. She was so very cold.

She waited for sleep that she knew wouldn't come, that had refused to come in the days since Jimmy Mino blurted out her fate. Instead, Fiona's mind, mercifully she thought, gave her flashes of Sully: an infant beside her on this very coverlet, enraptured with his toes; a feverish toddler, sucking his thumb and trusting her to cure him; a bullied boy, safe at home. He was present and alive, continually metamorphosing from newborn to boy and back again. She encircled this memory-child's sleeping, satisfied body.

A while later Nick's gentle knock pushed open the bedroom door. A rush of noise bounded into the room behind him—muffled voices punctuated by brash laughter, laughs that extinguished midway when the person remembered where he was. And underneath all that static, Fiona heard one word repeated again and again: *Sully*, until Nick latched the door and silence returned.

Nick's weathered hand slid a teacup and saucer onto her bedside table with a clink. Fiona did not acknowledge his presence and hoped that he would leave so she could return to Sully. She stared at the cup. It was an antique Spode that she had taken from her mother's cupboard on her last day in England. Probably worth something, Fiona thought. She had found it necessary both to take this fragile piece of her homeland and to do so secretively. Her mother would never have tolerated anything as soppy as carrying a porcelain memento across the Atlantic. Fiona wondered if her mother had ever missed this particular cup and saucer, and if she had suspected Fiona of being the type to take it.

Fiona smelled the distinct aroma of her favorite white tea steaming from the dainty cup: It was an emperor's luxury, made from new buds just before they opened. With its pale color, it hardly seemed tea at all to the uninitiated. Nick must have searched for it, Fiona realized. That morning she had pushed it to the back of the cabinet so the caterers wouldn't serve it to the hordes of guests who would scarf it down like

Tetley's. She never could forgive the American ignorance about tea. Nick's grandfather had been Turkish, and Nick had inherited only two things from him: eyes the color of fresh-tilled soil and a love for black coffee, bitingly bitter. Nick wouldn't touch the delicate tea that Fiona craved, but she didn't mind. At least he knew how to appreciate something rare.

Nick walked to the other side of the bed and lay on top of the blankets as Fiona had. He draped the quilt from the foot of the bed over them both and pressed himself against Fiona's back. He wrapped her skinny body in his arms, buried his head in her hair, and began to sob. She held onto his furry forearm, but no tears slid down her own face. Nick needed her; she knew this. He needed her to turn to him at that very moment and offer comfort. This, Fiona thought, was what she had vowed to do so long ago. Offer comfort: for better, for worse. So she tried, holding his heavy hand against her breast, but she could not roll to him. Her loss was private and solitary. She wanted it to be hers alone. After he fell asleep, she waited, relieved—not wanting to wake him—watching the sun move across the wisteria, listening as the screen door slammed shut on each departing mourner, as the kitchen staff cleaned the pots and pans and trays, as the vacuum sucked up the crumbs, and the refrigerator swallowed up a year's worth of leftovers sealed in tidy Tupperware.

ONE MONTH AFTER THE funeral, Nick rocked on the porch swing with his coffee and the Sunday *New York Times* while Fiona pruned the wisteria. The vine had taken advantage of her distraction during a month of growing season, and had bossily crept over the railing and transformed the porch into a lavender tree house.

"That musical Sully was rehearsing just opened," Nick said, dropping the paper onto his lap. He looked at Fiona over his reading glasses. "God, I miss him."

He pulled off the glasses and ground his knuckles into his eye sockets.

Fiona glimpsed the elderly man Nick was becoming. He was gray through the temples and bald at his crown, and his midsection, which had always been firm from a life of energetic construction work, now seemed paunchy. He looked like his father. How hadn't Fiona noticed this before? Nick was eleven years her senior, making him sixty-five this past March. She had always been attracted to the maturity and expertise his extra years gave him, especially when they met and she had been younger than Sully was at his death. Nick had stolen Fiona away from her mother and the stone cottage in the Cotswolds that he had been hired to repair, away from lemon curd, fish and chips, and team colors at the pub. He would take care of her, she had known, in the most literal of ways, and he always had, but he was beginning to wither into an old man.

Fiona looked down at the tender new growth she was pruning, each snip a careful choice, teaching the wisteria where it was allowed to go but without cutting away next year's blooms.

"Fee?"

Nick's watery eyes were on her; Fiona could feel them against her scalp like the scorch of the summer sun.

"I need to talk about him. I need to talk to you."

It wasn't the first time Nick had made this plea, and Fiona could sense his impatience. Still, no words seemed right. Should she say that she had lost Sully long before he had died? That she had lost him when he had found more love for that Hugo, or maybe for the boy before that, than for her? That she had mourned him before that horrific Friday morning. Should she say that talking about Sully now would only dilute what little she had left? She had no intention of sharing those shreds with Nick, whether he craved them or not. She clipped a few more shoots of the plant.

"Sully hated this wisteria," Nick sighed.

Fiona took in the wide porch with its woody shade, sheltering them from passersby.

"I wouldn't say that," said Fiona.

"No?" Nick snapped. "What would you say then?"

Fiona considered the fading blooms, browning a bit around the edges. The porch was already littered with petals, and the cloying smell of their decay made her queasy. Nick's intensity scared her, but she wouldn't let him rewrite the past as she knew it to be. Her future had already been snatched from her control, the past—the things she had devoted her adulthood to—wouldn't be tainted by his revisionism.

"There's lemon squash in the fridge," she said. "I'll get you some."

In the summer of his eighth year, Sully had become convinced that the wisteria would creep through his window in the middle of the heat-drenched night and suffocate him. Each morning he measured the tendrils seeking a new place to entwine. He stretched them along the edge of a tape measure Nick had given him for a failed father-son bonding project. Twenty-two and an eighth. Twenty-two and a half. Sully kept the data in a spiral notebook to prove his hypothesis.

"It's going to strangle me," he choked out through tears on his parents' bedroom floor in the middle of the night.

"Don't be so melodramatic. It's just a plant." Fiona brought him back to bed again and again.

For the years they had lived in the house, Fiona had been patiently training the wisteria up and across the shadier side of the house alongside Sully's bedroom. She had finally begun to be successful, and she wasn't going to give that up because Sully's imagination was overactive.

After a particularly hysterical night, Nick stopped midway through breakfast, a piece of toast punctuating the air, and said to Sully, "How about we take down the wisteria today?"

Fiona laughed, but Sully leapt to his feet. "Really? Could we really?"

"Yeah," said Nick, "if it bothers you so much." He turned to Fiona, "It's doing a number on the house anyway. We might as well."

"You can't be serious," said Fiona. "That plant has been living on this house for a century and it will be here long after us. We chose this house because of that wisteria. Absolutely not."

"I seem to recall being more taken with the solid construction myself," said Nick with a wink at Sully. Fiona slammed her knife onto the table.

They had bought the house when they were newly married and living in a dilapidated split-level on Route 18. They had lain in wait for more than three years to find an affordable antique house in Old Stonington that they could slowly refurbish. The wisteria house had been close to a tear-down. The prior owner, an elderly lady who had died in the front parlor, had left the house with a stench of Bengay and a burgeoning mold infestation. For the next decade— through Fiona's four miscarriages and Sully's miraculous birth, through burnt holiday roasts and lazy Sundays on the porch—Nick rebuilt the house. He brought in his electricians to strip out the knob-and-tube wiring and a plumber to replace the lead pipes. He repaired horsehair plaster that had separated from its lath, lovingly rehabilitated deteriorated window sashes, preserving their wavy glass. He sanded and polished the oak floors, repaired the slate roof, and duplicated with exactitude every inch of trim that had gone soft with rot and neglect.

The house became the best advertisement he could have had for his business, perched as it was at the head of Main Street. The Historic District Commission's darling. Not a detail overlooked. But Nick had gotten too tired (or too old, Fiona uncharitably thought), before he finished the upstairs, and

they ended up settling in just two rooms—theirs and Sully's—
with a utilitarian bathroom in between. The other three
bedrooms remained sealed off, still decrepit, their radiators
turned off to save on the heating bills. Fiona considered those
rooms her failures, knowing that had she managed to have
the four children they had planned, Nick would have found
the inner reserve to lovingly finish each one. But her womb
had proven recalcitrant, and she had been lucky to eke out
Sully. Fiona had almost forgotten the other rooms had ever
been there—were there still—just waiting.

"Can you really cut it down, Dad?" asked Sully.

Nick sat up in response to his son's admiration, a rarity
enough.

"No," answered Fiona. "Full stop."

She handed Sully a plate of scrambled eggs, and he pushed
them around in endless loops. Nick chewed the rest of his
toast and shrugged at his son.

Fiona could feel Sully's distress growing, the way she
once had been able to hear his infantile shrieks before they
had even started, as if her ears had special detectors for what
was budding within him. It was infuriating that Nick would
make her into the villain, claiming the white hat for himself.

"It's not fair, Mom," Sully finally yelled, his freckled brown
face flushing. "You love that stupid tree more than me."

His chair toppled over, and he ran upstairs, his slamming
door rattling the panes in the kitchen windows.

Fiona sighed. Nick perused the front page of the *Gazette*.

"You shouldn't give him crazy ideas," Fiona said.

Nick buried his head deeper in the paper, not
acknowledging the reprimand but not fighting it either. Years
before, they had reached a silent agreement, with Nick
surrendering to Fiona the final word with regard to all things
Sully. Fiona had struggled so much to carry a baby to term
that once Sully arrived she considered him a reward. Her
reward. She made excuses to Nick about why she alone

could hold him. He needs to nurse. He's teething. He's having separation anxiety. Nick returned to his renovations, and Fiona wove a bond around Sully that excluded Nick altogether. Fiona had liked to imagine Sully and Nick orbiting around her, like planets in a solar system, showered in her warmth, but not drawn to one another.

After finishing the breakfast dishes, Fiona retrieved her pruning shears from the shed. She found Sully still facedown on his pillow.

"I've been thinking, if you really want to tame that wisteria, you ought to get to work."

Sully sat up and searched Fiona's face for a trick. She presented the shears, "Here. I'll let you prune it."

"Okay," Sully said. He had to use both of his small hands to squeeze the shears closed.

"Be careful. If you lop off a finger, you'll have no one to blame but yourself."

"I will," he said and climbed out of his bedroom window onto the porch roof in only his pajamas.

For the next three hours, Sully was intent on his crusade, but the wisteria proved resilient. By lunch he had only a small heap of cuttings to show for his effort. While he ate his peanut butter and jam, his head drooping, Fiona surveyed the damage. The area near Sully's window looked a bit bedraggled but nothing the plant couldn't regrow by the end of the season. The wisteria's planned trek across Sully's side of the house would continue without disruption. Pleased to have calmed her son's anxiety without having to seriously damage her wisteria, Fiona suggested a conciliatory trip to the beach and then Macintyre's for an ice cream cone. Sully reluctantly agreed, and for the rest of the afternoon, he and Fiona built a sand city and pretended it was under siege by an army of cockleshells. But when she tucked him into bed that night, he said, "It's still out there."

"Well, it's a lot farther away from your window."

Sully rolled toward the wall.

"Don't be a goose," said Fiona, running her hand over his thick hair. "A knight wouldn't be afraid of a silly plant, you know. There are better things to worry about."

Sully said nothing, but the next day he ineptly nailed his windows shut, and for the rest of the summer he slept in a swelter, refusing the fan Fiona put at the end of his bed.

TEN MONTHS AFTER THE funeral, Fiona came home from a Garden Club meeting to find Nick packing up Sully's room. Other than dusting, not much had been done there since Sully had left for college more than a decade before. Its décor had become less and less appropriate each holiday he came home. His adult body struggled to fit in the plaid-sheeted twin bed. Posters from high-school drama productions cluttered the walls. Fiona had never been able to take anything down.

Nick had cleaned out Sully's New York apartment months earlier. Most of those things stayed with Hugo. The rest came home in a few discreet boxes. Nick sent the clothes to Goodwill and kept only the playbills and scripts. Fiona hadn't wanted any of it. The Sully she knew was still up in that room at the top of the stairs.

Fiona was startled when she saw Nick in Sully's room, partly because no one should be in there, but mostly because, sitting cross-legged on the floor, Nick looked remarkably like Sully, as if the room itself had the power to turn back time. Sully had had his father's lanky body, with legs that never seemed comfortable. But he was so much darker-skinned than either of his parents that when he was little Fiona was sometimes asked which adoption agency they had used. It was as if the Middle-Eastern blood that flowed diluted through Nick's body had been resurrected full-strength in his son. When he was a teen, Fiona had worried that Sully would feel ostracized in this whitest of towns. But he told his mother that she had it wrong. He had an advantage. "Everyone here thinks I'm exotic, but the rest of the world takes me as a mutt. I fit in with no one and everyone at the same time." And hadn't that been Sully, after all?

Fiona leaned against the doorframe. "I told you I wanted to do this."

"We should have turned this into a guest room when Sully went to college. It's like a time capsule."

"Don't smoke, Nick. You're making everything stink."

Nick exhaled a cloud toward the ceiling. He cracked the one window that hadn't been claimed by the wisteria. Outside, sounds of a new spring—kids screeching and snippets of cyclists' conversations—broke the silence. He placed his ashtray on the windowsill and left his cigarette, still lit, in it.

"Look at these old photo albums. I'd forgotten how many plays Sully was in." He flipped a few more pages. "Come sit with me."

"God, you've made a mess."

Fiona half-folded and half-tossed clothes still on their hangers into a box. She opened another box and started to pull more clothes out of the dresser.

Alternating between cigarette and beer, Nick flipped through a boyhood's worth of photos and then returned to the tall bookshelves and continued to neatly pile books into small boxes.

"Look at these novels. I didn't even know they wrote books for gay kids."

"Sully wasn't gay until he got to college. He went to the prom. Remember? And the senior ball."

Nick laughed. "Well, that certainly proves it." He sighed. "Just because we didn't want to see it doesn't mean it wasn't there. You know, I once found Morris and Sully down by the river kissing. They told me it was for their spring play and the boys had to be stand-ins because the girls' school couldn't make it to all the rehearsals. I actually believed that."

"Maybe it was true."

Nick laughed again. "You think?"

"You never told me that."

"No, I guess not." Nick stacked another layer of books into a box.

Fiona slammed the empty drawer closed. "It would have been nice to find out a decade earlier."

But she wasn't sure that was true. It had been hard enough when Sully was already an adult, already moved away. She had tried to be nonchalant and accepting the way people were supposed to be, but it hadn't been what she had imagined for him. For their family. What would it have been like if he had made some big proclamation over the lunch tables at the academy?

"Oh, come on." Nick sighed. "It was a long time ago."

"No wonder you were so bloody understanding when Sully came out. You had longer to get used to the idea."

Fiona wanted a fight, to prove some indefinable betrayal, but Nick wasn't interested. He sealed the box with strapping tape and marked it: Gay Teen Fiction. Fiona read the label and blinked. She tilted her head to get a better look at the other boxes Nick had prepared. Acting Guides. Philosophy. Gay Studies.

"Gay Studies?" she asked.

"Yeah, Sully had a box of bad self-help books on coming out under his bed."

Nick crushed out his butt and picked up two of the boxes. He struggled to get his footing and then, balanced, headed to the stairs.

"Where are you taking those?"

"To my truck."

"Why?"

"I'm bringing them over to the library."

"You can't do that."

"Why not? Aren't you always saying we should support Old Stonington's fine cultural institutions?"

"They put those books out in the boxes they were dropped off in."

"I know. That's why I labeled them. So they'll know what Dewey decimal number they are—or whatever else those zany librarians like to do."

"Gay studies? Gay fiction? Are you mad?"

"Yeah, I figured that would be a pretty exciting change for them."

"Everyone will know they're ours. Sully's. It's private."

"You don't think people know he was gay? Guess what, they do. Hell, they probably knew before you did. And do you really think Sully was the only gay kid in Old Stonington? Can't you get over it? He's gone, for Christ's sake."

"Put them down."

Nick turned his head toward the window. A garbage truck driving past made it impossible to speak for a moment. He dropped the two offending boxes at Fiona's feet. He took the other two and headed downstairs. Despite what Nick had said, Fiona didn't really think that no one knew about Sully. And she had gotten comfortable with Sully's sexual orientation for the most part, though she still sometimes thought of it as a bad habit he had picked up in college, like some kids do with smoking or drinking. But she didn't trust that her neighbors were quite so open-minded. It was their private business, after all, not up for chatter. Fiona listened for the kitchen screen door to slam, the truck to turn over, and gravel to crunch beneath its tires before she pushed the boxes back under Sully's bed.

THE AFTERNOON BEFORE THE accident Sully had arrived home unexpectedly. He leapt onto the porch and announced like a circus ringleader, "I have brought glad tidings!" In each hand he held a bottle of champagne. "Let's toast."

Fiona had laughed and clapped her hands together. "Sully, I'm so glad you're home."

She pulled off her gardening gloves and squeezed him. He seemed taller than she had remembered from a few months earlier, although she knew he had long stopped growing. And he had buzz-cut his black curls and dyed the stubble Marilyn Monroe blond.

"What did you do to your hair?"

"Like it?" he said, framing his face in his hands. "It's for a part. That's what we're going to celebrate."

Sully unwound the cage on the top of the champagne bottle and pulled the cork off with a flourish. He poured the wine in old juice glasses he grabbed from the draining board while Fiona searched the cabinets for flutes. "Life can't wait for proper crystal, Mom. It needs to be celebrated immediately."

They used the first bottle to toast his new part in the musical he'd been rehearsing. He'd been promoted out of the chorus to take over for some actor who'd managed to snag a lead in something better. When they had guzzled their way through that—with Sully bellowing a few bars of his new part's solo—he ran to the fridge and grabbed the second bottle. They ordered in Chinese to keep the celebration going and sat on the wisteria porch savoring the strange mix of hoisin sauce and dry wine. Sully ate slowly, as if the energy of his announcements had exhausted him.

"If I eat another morsel, I'll burst," said Fiona.

Nick handed out fortune cookies and snapped his in half. He was about to read it aloud when Sully interrupted.

"Wait," he said. "There's something else. Something I've wanted to say for a while but I didn't have the nerve." He stared at the unbroken cookie in his hands.

Nick moved closer to Fiona on the wicker settee.

"Don't be dramatic, Sully, whatever it is can't be that bad," Fiona said, but she knew otherwise. Sully usually, if anything, minimized bad news.

"We already know you're gay," blasted Nick, and he and Sully burst into gales of laughter. Fiona rolled her eyes in irritation at their drunken humor—like Sully's being gay was an inside joke for them. Nick's laughter didn't stop after the joke had passed.

"Seriously, though. This isn't good." Sully breathed deeply. "I'm HIV-positive." Nick and Fiona stared at him. "I know, I know. I'm not sure how it happened, but I've known for a while. I'm responding really well to the drug therapy. Hugo's been so supportive, and we just wanted you to know."

The champagne made Fiona's thoughts foggy. Through a blur she saw Sully's white hair and serious expression. She saw Nick's knee next to her own. She saw her pink-tipped fingers on the table. She blinked twice to clear her eyes.

"Are you dying?" she said, her voice breaking on the last syllable.

"Not today," Sully said with a soft laugh. Nick responded with a giggle of his own that he immediately stifled with a fake cough.

"What is wrong with you two?" Fiona turned to Nick, "He has AIDS. Were you listening?"

"Yeah, I'm listening. What I'm hearing is something that I can't change anyway."

Sully interrupted. "Actually, Mom, it's not AIDS. I'm just HIV-positive."

"Just? Don't be smart, Sully. I watch the news. You will die of this. Am I right?"

"Not necessarily," Sully said, the contrite schoolboy again.

Fiona could not contemplate Sully's dying. He could not die. He would not die. It had to be a mistake. No one gets AIDS anymore. She couldn't recall the last time she had seen an article in the paper. All those smart gay men knew how to protect themselves. Men like Hugo and Sully. And now her son was another statistic, while Hugo stood by blissfully virus-free. Fiona felt a surge of anger: at not having known before Hugo, at Sully's recklessness, at the shame of it all.

"It's too much, Sully. Do you have any other little surprises for us? Any more bottles of champagne in the fridge? What, do you have cancer? Have you won the bloody Nobel Peace Prize?" Fiona stood up abruptly, knocking over the carton of beef fried rice. Chopsticks spun across the floor. She reached for the porch banister and caught a wisteria vine instead.

"Mom, it'll be okay."

In Fiona's belly, too much alcohol and MSG and bad news churned together. She touched Sully's fuzzy blond head. She wanted to hug him like she had when he arrived, but she couldn't. Not right now.

"I can't think," she said.

"Don't worry. It's going to be fine. I just wanted you to know. I need to know that you both are with me."

"Of course we are," said Nick. "Whatever you need."

"Mom?"

"Oh, Sully. What more do you want from me?"

SIXTEEN MONTHS AFTER SULLY died, the Old Stonington Historical Society had its fall charity auction. Fiona and Nick went every year but never bid on anything because it was too expensive. When Sully was in high school, Fiona had talked him and a few of his friends from the academy chorus into bidding themselves out to perform Christmas carols at a holiday party. All winter Fiona received compliments on the boys' performance. She had asked Sully to sing the carols for her and Nick, but he never quite got around to it. Those boys were always so busy.

Usually one of the ladies from the society would call or stop by to sell the auction tickets, but last year no one had because of Sully's death. Fiona supposed that this year they must not have made it back onto the list, or maybe she and Nick were still supposed to be relieved of social obligations. It annoyed Fiona that those social mavens thought they could dictate how, and for how long, she should mourn. So she bought tickets from the girl at the information desk instead of calling a neighbor. She went to her favorite dress shop a few towns over and spent more money than what she had paid for the tickets to buy the perfect gown, a decidedly happy fuchsia silk without a hint of mourning. It clung to her trim figure, and a little row of hanging beads at the hem danced around her legs.

The night of the auction, she laid out Nick's tuxedo, its black having lost some of its sheen but still fitting well enough. He would wear the cufflinks that Fiona had given him on their first anniversary, back when she had hoped he might study law like his father or maybe become an architect since he loved construction so much. Now the cufflinks only made appearances at weddings or fundraisers.

"Are you nearly ready?" she hollered down the stairs.

It had been so long since she and Nick had gone out like this. Even though it was only an auction, more a chore really than a festive occasion, Fiona enjoyed feeling pretty again, eager for a compliment. But Nick didn't look up when she finally came downstairs, just grabbed his keys from the hall table and said, "Let's go."

"Oh, right." Fiona smoothed her skirt.

Nick drove faster than necessary, and when he should have made the left onto Macgowan Road, he instead veered onto Route 18.

"It's at the club," said Fiona.

Nick said nothing and finally stopped ten minutes later in a wooded turnout beside the town reservoir. Moonlight reflected off the water. He stepped from the car, and Fiona reluctantly followed. She rubbed her arms, the flimsy dress offering no protection against the chill.

"Have you been out here at all?" Nick said. "Even once? The Judge and I fished the reservoir a dozen times this summer. Even a few times last year."

Fiona could picture the two aging men, waddling around in their hip-waders, their easy laughter echoing off the water.

Nick pointed across the reservoir to where a small dam held back the water. Fiona knew, though she had assiduously avoided the spot, that by the dam Route 18 dropped steeply downhill and made a sharp right turn. Years ago a child had been paralyzed after her brakes failed on the hill and she launched herself into the stony creek. Old Stonington had erected a concrete barrier after that, but Fiona had always wondered how this would have possibly changed the outcome for that poor child. She knew, too, that Sully's jeep had hit that wall head-on.

"He was going fast, Fee. Really fast."

Fiona felt something savage filling up her gut and crushing her lungs and wrapping around her throat.

"Is this necessary?" she said.

"Yes, it is. I can't keep acting like we're all fine. Going off to some goddamned fundraiser like we're all okay. I won't do it anymore."

The whole time he spoke, Nick dug his hands deep into his trouser pockets, and he looked across the water like he was telling all this to the Judge out there with his rod and reel. He probably had done just that, Fiona realized, practiced this whole horrible speech on that old man.

"We're going to be late," said Fiona.

"You're unbelievable. That's all you've got?"

And then she said, "You shouldn't have let him leave." And as the words fell, she realized that this was exactly what she had been feeling for more than a year, every time she looked at Nick's face, every time he brought her tea or sat beside her or asked her if he could help with dinner.

"You think this is my fault? Jesus, listen to yourself. You know your son better than that. Sully knew just what big dramatic statement he wanted to make, and he made it."

"You could have stopped him."

"What about you? Why do you think he was out here in the first place? Who was that performance for?"

Four years later, on a bitter Halloween night, Fiona and Nick ate caramel apples and handed out cheap chocolate to the hordes of vampires and Power Rangers that stormed up the front steps under the shriveled wisteria. Each year there were more kids walking the historic district for treats; their own rural roads making candy collection too onerous. Fiona had given out ten bags this year, most of which she figured would either make the kids sick or would wisely be thrown away in a few days by their mothers.

"Do you remember the year that Sully decided to be Henry VIII for Halloween?" Fiona said.

Nick nodded. "That costume you made was a perfect replica. I'm sure the other moms were annoyed at you until Christmas for that one."

"It's what Sully wanted."

"That's all, huh?"

"Maybe you're right. I had too much time on my hands." She twirled the caramel in loops around the apple trying to stretch it apart. "But you have to admit he looked spectacular."

"Yes, he did."

When the trick-or-treaters' parade became only a handful of teenagers with cheap drugstore masks, their already-deepened voices too manly to be begging for candy, Fiona and Nick built a fire in the living room and ate leftover peanut-butter cups and chianti. He handed her an envelope.

"What's this?" said Fiona, laughing and pleased.

"Open it."

Inside were two plane tickets to London. It had been a dozen years since she'd been back; the last time had been for her mother's funeral.

"I thought we could go for Christmas," Nick said. "Start a new tradition. What do you say?"

Fiona nodded. "It's lovely. Really." But how she could she not be home to set up a tree in the front window as they always had? How could she miss the chance to conjure, just for that night, every holiday incarnation of Sully, like joyful little nesting dolls? And there were all the little British traditions that she had made theirs—Christmas crackers and plum pudding. They were special here in Old Stonington but would be ordinary in England. Only at the big holidays could Fiona conjure, for even an ephemeral moment, a living Sully, not just the two-dimensional memory of photographs. She said, "I need to think about it."

Nick leaned back into his chair and finished his wine in a gulp. "Sometimes thinking gets in the way."

A DECADE AFTER SULLY'S DEATH, Fiona called a horticulturist to look at the wisteria. Once the summer foliage had dropped, she had noticed a strange green fungus. In places the bark was even peeling away, exposing the raw inside of the trunk. Much of the growth from the last year was already brown and shriveled.

The horticulturist wore a white jumpsuit like a doctor in an isolation ward. He crawled in the dirt around the bases of the wisteria, one at each of four pillars that framed the front steps. The woody branches intertwined into a rope measuring nearly a foot in diameter. He scraped samples of the fungus and examined them under a magnifying glass in his van.

"Well, this fungus has probably been growing here for years and years. Yeah, it happens sometimes. Real shame. An old plant like this—you know, most people don't realize this—but they've got a lifespan just like a person. There comes a day when it just can't get any bigger, or sometimes the soil's been sucked dry. Whatever the reason, the plant weakens. Then a big storm or just some little parasite can knock it right out. I'm sorry, ma'am, but your wisteria needs to come down."

"But most of it's still healthy."

The horticulturist shrugged. "Maybe if you had caught it earlier. Who knows? But not now." He looked at the house and sighed as if distressed at Fiona's lack of foresight. "Hate to see such a beautiful specimen go. We'll take it down gently. Won't damage the house much either. It could be pretty bad under there."

"Thanks, anyway," she said. "I'll take it down myself."

He nodded in understanding.

But, of course, in the end Fiona couldn't touch the wisteria, so she asked Nick to do the deed. He said he'd need to bring in some of his guys to help with the higher spots. Nick had stopped using ladders now that his balance was unreliable. He sent Fiona to Nantucket for a cold November weekend. On a beach where sky, sand, and sea melted into a monochromatic horizon, Fiona waited for the job to be done. Nick called her late on Sunday afternoon.

"Can I come home now?" she asked.

"Yes. But be prepared for a huge change," said Nick. "It wasn't easy taking that thing down. It did some serious damage."

When she returned, the only reminder of the wisteria were two stumps at the foot of the pillars. The house was naked and badly in need of repair. And Nick had moved his drafting table and himself to the Judge's guesthouse.

Every few days, Fiona packed another box of clothes or mementos that Nick had left behind so she would have an excuse to visit him at his office. He was always pleasant enough to her, but she couldn't find a way to ask why he was gone. She supposed she should know. That he would sigh the way he did when she wasn't seeing what was apparently obvious to everyone else. But from Fiona's view, he had been there and then he was gone.

Nick said he had more business than he could handle. "Busier than I've been in years." Blueprints and coffee cups covered every horizontal surface. The phone rang, and he smiled at Fiona apologetically. As he bellowed away at a wayward subcontractor, she watched thirty years of aging blow away. Nick covered the mouthpiece and said, "Sorry."

As Christmas loomed, Fiona couldn't begin to imagine recreating the usual set piece of decorations. The boxes sat in the attic, and Fiona told herself that she'd begin decorating the next day. Or the next. Then, on the day of the Garden Club Greens Sale, a wreath with a crushed, garish, red velvet bow appeared on her door, hung from the brass knocker. Nick, she thought. But when the handwriting on the outside of the envelope was unfamiliar she assumed one of the Main Street ladies had been annoyed at her lack of festive decorations and was trying to give her a hint. How many times had Fiona heard her neighbors say that the whole Old Stonington community counted on the antique houses in the village center to set the holiday mood? But to her surprise the note said, *Merry Christmas from the Minos.* Fiona tried to reshape the bow but it stayed flattened from having been stacked in a pile. It didn't matter, she decided. From a distance it looked just fine.

A week before Christmas, Fiona taped a plane ticket to London on Nick's door with a card that said simply, *Please come.* Even that had been difficult to write. She looked at the matching ticket pinned to her corkboard every time she answered the phone. But no call came. Instead Nick sent an email saying he was tied up on a project for the Judge, converting his back barn into a painting studio for his wife as a Christmas present. He offered to pay her back for his ticket. He hoped she would go without him and visit her old friends. *Love, Nick.*

When they ran into each other at the hardware store in January, Fiona told him that she had gone to the West End to see the same musical Sully had been rehearsing all those years back. That it had been stupendous. Hilarious. It would have been better with Sully, of course. That her sister sends love. She might come over in the spring. That it was as dreary over there as ever, no hope of a white Christmas.

"Well, we didn't get one this year, either. Just some sleet."

"I guess I didn't miss much," said Fiona, not meaning it.

Before she could find another topic, Nick excused himself and left the store empty-handed. Fiona tried not to think about that on her way back home. That night she turned on the radiators in Sully's room and the living and dining rooms and filled the house with the soundtrack from Sully's play. She could do things like this now, she told herself. Crazy, foolish, impractical things, and no one was there to object.

Sixteen years, four months, and several days after Jimmy Mino had pulled up in his cruiser at dawn, Fiona called a realtor. The house sold quickly, but not for as much as she'd hoped. Of course, it needed work. Of course, it would do better if she had it painted. Nick would have had all of that taken care of, but she wouldn't speak to him about any of it. The realtor pressed her to just clean up the clutter in the extra bedrooms to help the house seem more alive. "You're selling a fantasy, you see," she said gently. "You want them thinking, if I buy this house, my life will be just like theirs." *God forbid,* thought Fiona. An idealistic couple bought the house anyway, with big dreams and an ample checkbook. Fiona supposed she wasn't allowed to see them, but she waited around the corner when they came for their inspection. The wife was fit and blonde like every other young mother in Old Stonington nowadays. They had a little girl—all fairy wings and ringlets— who kept leaping off the wisteria stumps while her parents cooed over the house's façade.

As the closing drew near, Fiona emptied the house from attic to cellar. She hired Jimmy Mino's son to come over one weekend to fill a dumpster. He refused her check. "My dad says if there's anything you ever need, Mrs. Faydah, just call him . . ." Fiona couldn't decide if this was pity or friendship.

Her car loaded to the gunnels, Fiona remembers to stop at the grocery store to pick up a few things before the storm blows in. She is inspecting a shelf of poinsettias for the least spindly one—there hasn't been time with all the packing to make it to the greenhouse—when she spots Nick at the refrigerated case.

They exchange pleasantries the way they have learned to do over the years. She mentions a few outstanding issues from the house closing. He hadn't wanted his share of the proceeds, and when she mentions it now, he glances down at his crumpled shopping list. "Anyway," he says, ignoring her comments about banker's checks, "I'm really glad you got a good price. Sorry I couldn't help out more, but looks like you knew what you were doing more than me. I build 'em, not sell 'em."

They both laugh and Fiona can hear a little rattle in Nick's chest. All that secretive smoking finally catching up to him, she supposes. From a distance Nick had looked the same as always, but up close she notices how wrinkled he is and how his Adam's apple seems to poke out more than it used to. But he still seems strong and sturdy in a way that Fiona, at seventy, hasn't felt in years. Instead, she worries daily about how brittle her bones have become and how much her skin has sagged despite science's best efforts. At night, she lies in bed trying to remember how to sleep through the night. Fiona wishes she had been more careful with her makeup that morning, but she hadn't bothered when she was going to spend the day cleaning house. She thought how dreadful she must look.

"I've rented a little cottage from that new family on Riverview," she says. "You'll have to stop by to see it. Maybe on Boxing Day?"

"Maybe. I'll let you know about that."

In the ensuing pause, Fiona scans Nick's basket for some evidence of loneliness, but finds only spaghetti sauce, milk, and bread.

"They're saying it's going to snow tonight," she says. Nick has always loved a good storm.

"So I heard," Nick nods. "I should probably get going." He begins to push his cart toward the check-out line.

"I heard eighteen inches," Fiona says, raising her voice a little. Her forecast echoes the hundreds of others she and Nick listened to on the TV or radio from some overeager weatherman during more than thirty years of marriage. And in a flash, the grocery store disappears, and Fiona sees her family again, in the kitchen, Nick telling her and Sully the latest snow totals, guessing the likelihood of a snow day.

Nick smiles as if he sees it, too. "That much, huh?"

"Maybe twenty."

"Well, I've got a plow on the truck this year so you give me a call if you need help digging out."

He rests his hand atop Fiona's on the handle of her cart. Its weight warms her cold fingers like a woolen blanket in a January bedroom. A blush of pleasure races to her cheeks. "Thanks for offering," she says and, then, with habitual politeness. "I'm sure I'll be fine."

"I've never doubted that, Fiona. But I'll try to stop by anyway if the snow's bad, just in case."

Fiona loads her groceries into the station wagon and drives slowly down Main Street, past Sully's nursery school and the library, past their old house soon to have its new people, to the little in-law cottage the realtor had found for her to rent. She brews a pot of tea and settles by the bay window in the front room, impatiently watching the sky for the first flakes as the gloaming passes into night.

Jennifer Wisner Kelly grew up in Connecticut, where most of the stories in *Stone Skimmers* are set. Her work has appeared in *Poets & Writers*, *Greensboro Review*, *Massachusetts Review*, and *Beloit Fiction Journal*. She is a graduate of Harvard, University of Chicago Law School, and Warren Wilson College's MFA program. She now lives in Concord, Massachusetts and practices law at a domestic violence advocacy nonprofit. *Stone Skimmers* is her debut book.